MACMILLAN CARIBBEAN WRITERS

The Girl with the Golden Shoes

Colin Channer

MACMILLAN
CARIBBEAN

Macmillan Education
Between Towns Road, Oxford, OX4 3PP
A division of Macmillan Publishers Limited
Companies and representatives throughout the world

www.macmillan-caribbean.com

ISBN: 978-0-230-02892-0

Typeset by EXPO Holdings
Cover design and illustration by Tim Gravestock

Printed and bound in China

2012 2011 2010 2009 2008
10 9 8 7 6 5 4 3 2 1

I.

They were sitting on old buckets, scaling fish beneath an almond tree, when someone pointed to the water and they all began to shout.

They were hardy children who'd been raised in isolation on a crescent beach below a cliff, and had experienced many horrors – drownings, stabbings, births and storms. But when they saw a one-eyed monster rising from the deep, they dropped their tools and dashed off in a blur of skirts and faded tunics to the clump of shacks in which they lived, raising clouds of sand as white as salt.

The eldest girl, Estrella Thompson, would be fifteen soon, and thought herself mature. She'd recently begun to read, which had created an awareness of a universe beyond San Carlos. So, unlike her friends, she was interested in the war.

The war was taking place in Europe, a place she'd only heard about the year before. Poland. Antwerp. Riga. Spain. The names were sparkling gems of sound that shimmered with a range of possibilities that went beyond the dreams of all her neighbours in the cove. So on the rare occasions that she'd had the chance to travel into town, she'd steal away to loiter in the little shops in Woodley, the district of the artisans adjacent to the port. There, she'd listen to the intonations of the BBC announcer on the redifusion box and be transported like a person who'd gone to see a medium for a glimpse of life across the void into the other world.

On these nights more than others, as she curled up in the hammock she shared with other girls beneath a shed beside her old grandmother's hut, Estrella would gaze outside the window as she fingered old newspapers and her cache of stolen books, dreaming of the day when she'd be rescued from this place where nothing happened.

So while the others ran, she hid behind the almond tree and watched in fearful fascination as the creature loomed.

It wasn't until the mask had been removed that Estrella, who'd never been to school or travelled much on her tiny island, understood that what she thought had been a monster was a human being – a scuba diver in a rubber suit.

She stepped out from behind the tree and walked towards him in her old blue frock with eyelet lace around the hem, hips moving widely underneath the faded fabric, giving insight to the marvel of her shape. She was tall and big-boned with mannish shoulders and a long face with sharp cheeks. Her eyes were bright and slanted, and although her skin was darker than a Coke, she had a length of wavy hair.

"What are you wearing?" she asked in English, which she rarely had the need to use, since everyone around her spoke *Sancoche*.

"It lets me breathe beneath the water."

They talked for several minutes, during which he explained some of his duties; then he disappeared below the surf.

In *Sancoche*, her native dialect, Estrella kept repeating as the ripples disappeared, "I never even thought to dream of seeing a thing like that."

II.

"You can go on with you stupidness."

Two days had passed, and Tucker Ross had heard the story many times from many people, but most often from the girl, his granddaughter by the common law.

"Big Tuck," she said, insistently, "is true."

He fanned as if her words were buzzing insects.

"A man can't breathe underwater no matter what he put on his body or his head, Estrella. I really think is a mermaid you see. It have different kinds, you know. And I heard it have some that look like man, in truth."

They'd just completed dinner, and Estrella, who'd replayed her visitation many times, had told the story once again, with every detail in its place – the fellow was a blue-eyed Yankee soldier, and he'd told her he was part of something called "man hoovers", which meant he and some other men were practising a thing they had to do. And the thing they had to practise was to stick a thing like dynamite on German boats below the waterline and blow them up.

The night was hot, and she was sitting on a woven mat beneath the hut in which she lived with Big Tuck and her grandmother, Roselyn – a dark, thick-featured woman with a golden tooth that twinkled when she talked.

Roselyn had arrived in San Carlos in the 1920s from Havana, but she wasn't Cuban. She was a Trinidadian who'd gone to work in Cuba as a *waitress* in the early 1900s, brooding as she served her body to the Yankee soldiers stationed on the island to secure it in the nom de guerre of freedom – whose baptismal name is profit – after the Spanish–American War.

If she could, she would've returned to Trinidad; but word had travelled to her mother that she was a prostitute; and her mother, who for years had kept Roselyn's children, sent a message that she'd bought a special cricket bat to beat them nasty ways out of her dirty, worthless daughter if she ever came to Trinidad again.

When Roselyn moved to San Carlos, she'd left a daughter behind, a daughter born in Havana ... father unknown. Years later, when this daughter died in labour, Roselyn went to Cuba for her newborn child.

Almost dead at birth, that child, Estrella Thompson, grew up to be advanced beyond her years.

Like the other dwellings in the camp, the hut was roofed in thatch and set at shoulder height on wooden stilts. On the hottest evenings, Estrella and her family would eat below it on the shaded sand, which had been shielded from the heat.

"Is not stupidness," she offered in the rumbling cadence of *Sancoche*. "It have a lot o' things going on in this world we ain't know 'bout up here down this coast. Even in town things going on. Is only we don't know nothing. All we know is fish. Catch fish. Scale fish. Eat fish. Fry fish."

Big Tuck sat with his belly pressing on his dark brown shirt. He was squat and hairy, with skin the orange-brown of rum; and his chest and arms were bulky still from rowing boats and pulling nets for almost all his eighty years.

"I ain't disbelieve you when you say you see what you say you see," he told her in a silly voice that made her younger cousins giggle and her old grandmother laugh. "But all I know is that a man can't breathe underwater no matter what he put on. I ain't have to go to no school to know that."

"You know from the other day she start to read she getting different," Roselyn said with a gentle tease. "She start to know everything – even things that nobody ain't suppose to know until they dead. Because is only when you dead you can see certain

4

things. I ain't think it was a mermaid at all. I think she dead in truth and see a ghost."

"When she tell me that she teach herself to read, I frighten," said Big Tuck with admiration. He tapped Estrella's leg and handed her a cigarillo and his flask of rum.

"Tuck, she's a child, you know. She ain't suppose to drink no rum. It ain't have any beer?"

"Rose, you ain't see she's a woman? Leave the blasted child alone."

"Tuck," implored Estrella, smiling at him warmly, as she smoked and took a swig. "Look how long I tell you send me to school. But you only want keep me here to fish."

"Estrella," he replied, easing Roselyn from his lap and taking on a more attentive pose, "if you was in town right now, and the boss man come and ask you what kind o' work you want to do, what you would tell him, in truth?"

"I ain't know what kind o' work there is," Estrella answered promptly. "But I could work in a shop or in the bank. As long as you could count, you could do them kind o' things. How hard them work could be more than selling fish? Things is things. If you could sell one thing you could sell another thing, as long as you know how it measure, and how much a measure is the price. And most things they sell in these shops ain't have to measure. They just sell off a shelf one by one. All I would have to do is put them in a bag, make sure I give the right change, and don't insult nobody, which to me might be the hardest part, because in truth it have some people who will agitate you nerves."

"Is where you getting these thoughts?" her grandmother asked. A tone of slight concern had seeped into her voice.

"I have it in my head long time to do something, Grandma. But I just ain't get the chance to even know what I could do. How I going to know? Who going tell me? Them people here?"

She gestured broadly. "I ask the fellow that was doing man hoovers what I could do if I leave here, and he tell me I could do anything if I only put my mind."

"So," her grandmother said, "you let a stranger tell you what to do with you life?"

"You know it have a lot o' educated dunces in this world," Big Tuck pointed out. "Take Rawle boy. They send he away to university in the mother country and I hear he ain't pass no exam. I hear is bare zero he getting up at the place there ..." He paused to find the word. "Camron or Campton or Cam Ditch or some *rass*. That and Oxfam is the two biggest school they have in England they say. What kind o' man get opportunity like that and come back with two long hand and no qualification ... no doctor ... no engineer ... no barrister? That is why I keep myself right here. Rawle ain't know the white man school hard like brick or he wouldn't gone and fail. And he a white man too. Me? I stick with what I know. The fish in my blood. And Estrella, it in *your* blood too. If you let that go is death."

"If I stay here and don't do nothing with myself then that would kill me worse," she blurted, adding childish frills along her intonation. For although Big Tuck was funny, he was quick to take offence. And when he was upset he could be cruel.

They ain't understanding what I trying to say, Estrella thought. But maybe I should keep it to myself.

She'd not been led to reading by a great ambition – that was something reading had produced. But this wasn't easy to explain.

A year before, in 1941, on a market trip to the capital, Seville, she'd wandered off while running errands, and had taken up a spot across the street from La Sala de Amor to watch the cars arriving with the idle wives of businessmen and English civil servants.

La Sala, as Carlitos knew it, was the first of many mansions on the Queensway to be sold for business use. It was large and white, with thick limestone columns; and between the columns ran a lacy banister whose loops and swirls in black conferred a lingerie allure to anyone who dined on the veranda, basking in the currents driven by the celebrated fan, an engineering marvel that was bolted to the ceiling and whose giant wings, which had been woven in the previous century from a fibre that grew only in the Yucatán, made slow, gigantic swoops.

The Queens, as people called it, was an upward-sloping mile that started at a square beside the harbour and ended at the governor's imposing gate.

In Spanish times it had been known as the Paseo, and was the site of much parading by the rich. In its centre was a flowered median lined with rows of royal palms, curving trails with benches made of heavy wood, and gas-illuminated globes that seeped a misty sentimental light.

That day, as she watched the wives arriving for their lunch, Estrella recognised a chauffeur as a man who often bought fish from her grandmother, and she tried to make a sale.

"Oyi!" she shouted from a bench beneath a tree. "It have some good jack and parrot today. Nice bonito too. I save up some for you. When you finish you should come."

With his finger quickly brought across his lip, the man, whose job was marked by nothing more official than a visor, tossed his head, inviting her to cross the street. There, he introduced her to another driver as "the smartest little girl you'll ever meet".

"What kind o' woman you calling little girl?" the man replied. He wore a pith helmet and an ivory jacket with a scarlet sash.

"She overgrow," the man she knew remarked. "Overgrow and overripe."

"Is the fish she eating make her bottom juicy so?"

While the drivers talked about her as if she wasn't there, Estrella watched the people on the grand veranda, dreaming, and by accident observed something designed to be unseen.

When a husband moved across the veranda to greet a friend who'd just arrived, a waiter slipped his wife a note that had been scribbled by another man, a quiet diner seated by himself across the aisle.

The reaction to the written word was something that the girl had never seen. The lady's face, which before the note had been as plain and inexpressive as an egg, began to crackle with a smile.

It was a smile that wasn't triggered by the mouth, that only ended there, that looked as if it had begun somewhere inside the woman's liquid core. And that was when Estrella knew that writing was an elemental force, like hurricanes and floods, and began to visualise the stream of words she'd like to share with someone she loved.

That very day, she stole the first of many books, a language primer slid beneath the skirt along an aisle in McSweeney's, followed by a lesson here and there in phonics for a penny, which she took on credit from an eight-year-old girl who worked behind the counter in her father's Chinese shop.

However, in the weeks that followed her encounter with the diver, Estrella's greatest problem wasn't books. It was the *Star*.

Before she'd begun to read, the daily paper was a thing – a thing a mother used to line the box she turned into a cradle; a thing a child would fold to make a hat when it would rain; a thing that everybody used to wipe their bottoms; a yellow thing you picked out of the garbage when you went to town; a thing for everyone to use.

But in the weeks that followed her encounter, Estrella had begun to keep some papers for herself.

Because no one believed her story, she began to read the papers with the single-minded effort of a lawyer on the quest for vindicating proof. And to her family and neighbours, it appeared as if she'd pulled away.

It unsettled them to watch her reading ... smiling to herself ... whispering fancy words ... her finger pointing all the time ... her head bowed like she praying to the damn *rass* thing.

If you play you drum or pluck you *cuatro* when the gal was reading one, she'd walk away. What kind o' thing is that? And when she come back after she done walk away and you ask her what it really have inside that thing, she only want to tell you things 'bout other places – like where we from ain't place.

So although they were amazed that one of them had learned to read, they also felt as if the girl had put them under siege, a sense that if they didn't act, then history would remember them as people who'd watched and waited while their way of life was slowly laid to waste.

As days turned into weeks, Estrella found herself preparing fish beneath the almond tree alone. People whispered. When they had too much to drink sometimes, they'd lob their blazing words.

Is them things you reading in them papers have you head so tie up. You think we born big so we ain't know how children can be devious? If is you dead mother telling you things to come and confuse us, well, is a good thing she gone.

Intimidated by their parents and confused, the children who'd been with Estrella when the diver waded from the surf began to doubt what they'd seen. Pressured by his parents, a boy began to spread the rumour that Estrella had confided that the story was a hoax. Two girls swore on a Bible that they'd seen a mermaid flopping on the shore, long hair, gold comb and all. But most of them just shook their heads when asked and mumbled that they didn't know, that yes, they were there, but didn't see, that so much time had passed.

Through all of this, Estrella found a way to manage. But when her younger cousins, candid children, told her that it might be

9

better if she went away, she left the hammock where she slept with them and made a bed inside the broken body of an old canoe left rotting just outside a cave, fifty yards beyond the almond tree.

While this was happening in San Carlos, a tepid winter in the North Atlantic caused a shift in ocean streams all around the world, and the swimming patterns of the fish in the West Indies were disrupted for six weeks.

Each island had its range of local explanations. But in *this* corner of *this* island, there was only one. And after forty days of empty nets, the elders called a meeting on a desert cay.

"Big Tuck," the meeting started, "there's a problem in you house, and as a man you have to fix it."

They were sitting in a circle by a sea grape tree whose twisted branches formed a dome.

"Is not you flesh," they argued when he told them that he couldn't do what they were asking. "Everybody else who live here in some way or other is blood. The fish in we blood and it not in hers. And you is the very one that say she look you in you face and tell you right in front o' Rose that if she stay here she going dead."

"Well, that ain't what she say exactly," said Big Tuck, who had true, natural feelings for the girl.

"Tuck, what the *rass* you talking 'bout? This is forty days o' judgement. Forty days o' blight. The only time I see people round here holding they head like they ain't know if they coming or going was that long time when Mount Diablo look like it was going blow. Tuck, when you old like we you have to accept that we could see the signs. And every man in this place here seeing the signs right now. And you is one o' we, Tuck, so you bound to see them too."

10

"You ain't have to say nothing like that," Big Tuck replied. He took another drink, but couldn't keep it down. "You ain't have to test me if I is one o' you. I is one o' you in truth."

He wiped the trace of spit and vomit from his mouth.

"Is you bring Rose here to live," someone accused. "And is Rose bring she here. And Rose own story is a mix-up too. She born in Trinidad, then she gone and live in Cuba, then she come here with a baby saying the mother die in childbirth and no father ain't there. Tuck, how so much mix-up going on in you house?"

"You see sign?" the one who'd mentioned the volcano pointed out. "The gal kill she own mother. What she would do to we?"

"Tuck, if you get the feeling that you ain't able to manage," said the oldest one among them, "put the pressure 'pon you wife."

On the morning that she had to ask the girl to leave, Roselyn passed the line of huts belonging to her neighbours and walked into the water till it caught her at the knees. She was dressed in white, a flowing dress with puffed sleeves and a turban. In her ears there was a pair of silver hoops.

In a calabash gourd lined with a swatch of gingham cloth in white and blue, she'd placed some silver coins, red flowers, a watermelon slice and a jar of molasses. And as the gourd bobbled on the waves, she sang hymns to Yemoja asking the *orisha* for prosperity and safety for the girl.

The neighbours watched her furtively, peering through their barely open shutters and the cracks between the boards that made their huts, unhappy but relieved as Roselyn heaved her heavy body past the anchored, striped canoes, then came upon the almond tree, where she stopped for a moment before running back into the sea to put her earrings in the calabash.

"My heart feel like it going to burst," she told Estrella when the deed was done. "But since you curse the fish is only blight. Why you had to spit in God face? Now, he giving everybody bad eye."

Sitting on the edge of her broken canoe with her elbows on her knees, Estrella answered with a quiet pledge: "One day I going come back here and all o' you going look at me and frighten. That's all I have to say."

Square-jawed and trembling, Roselyn put her hands across her ears and heaved away.

"I not going live and dead in no shack in no place where nothing don't happen," said Estrella, standing up to shout. "Mark my words. Something big going happen to me. And you lucky you even find me anyway. You lucky you find me here this morning. I already make up my mind to leave this place ... to go my own damn way. And that ain't no jest. That's the gospel truth."

In the hut, Roselyn did as she'd promised Tuck the night before. She lay down on the bed beside him, listened to his snores, and took a dose of poison that would kill her in her sleep.

Later, during the hour of siesta, while Big Tuck and all the neighbours found it hard to sleep, Estrella sat beneath the hut to pack her things. She didn't have a lot, but she couldn't take it all, because she didn't have a bag. So she packed what she could carry in a basket, which she slung across her body with a length of rope, unaware, like Big Tuck and all the neighbours, that Roselyn was dead.

As she walked along the empty beach, Estrella felt the glare of eyes, which encouraged her to fortify her walk with more authority and grace. She pulled back her shoulders and stuck out her ass, and used a hand to dab at any hairs that might have loosened in her plaits.

When she came upon the almond tree, unsure of what would happen and wondering what to do – she'd never seen a person being banished in her life – she saw two fellows sitting in a red canoe.

"Hey, Estrella. How you doing? Come here. I want to talk to you."

"Come where?" she answered with a knowing look.

She stood, arms folded, water lapping at her shins.

"Well, it look like you going out. I just was thinking to ask you if you want a ride."

"Don't fret 'bout me, Alston. I could take care on my own."

She spat in punctuation, cut her slanted eyes and stomped away.

"Estrella. Where you going? Come back here. It ain't have no other way."

"Leave me alone."

"You have to come, Estrella. Make it simple. Don't make it turn a fuss."

She spun around.

"If I had my own boat is one thing. But I ain't going nowhere with the likes o' you. I would rather climb the cliff."

"Well go, nuh. See, nuh. Climb the cliff and break you neck and dead."

"Alston, you is a blasted dog."

As she stomped in the direction of the cliffs, she thought: How I could sit in a boat with Alston and Perry and act like nothing ain't happen? Them is fellows I know all my life. I know them men children. Them men even put talks to me a few times when their wife wasn't about. And in truth, I even do a little feel-up with that Alston there one time. Man is man, eh. After all o' that, he expect me to go with them in a boat so they could carry me

13

'way like I is some piece o' filth? Before I go with them I'd rather climb this cliff and get my death. Then what they going to say?

The limestone cliff was high and sheer, a little under ninety feet and flecked with blinking crystals. In certain spots, the roots of hardy plants came dangling out of fissures in the rock, and as she climbed, Estrella Thompson, who was too scared to look below, felt around with shoeless feet for little gaps or sills to hold her weight.

Hand over hand, her body taut with dogged anger, her sweating face so deep in focus that it was serene, slipping once or twice, she reached the top.

Without looking down to see the depth from which she'd come, or stare in triumph at her neighbours, who'd spilled out from their huts across the sand, the tall, strong-bodied girl began to sprint across a field of guinea grass towards the world she thought contained her future, moving through the gulf of green as swiftly as a marlin that had snapped a fishing line.

She wore a purple dress with long sleeves and puffed shoulders that were fraying at the seams. In her deep patch pockets bounced her gutting knife and money that she'd stolen from Old Tuck.

With fifteen pounds and fifty pence, she planned to buy a pair of shoes, the first ones in her life; after this, she would present herself correctly for a job.

III.

Like a beetle on a trail of gum, the stubby, silver bus was crawling north along the wild Atlantic coast. Estrella stared outside the window, a strong out-pointed cheekbone pressed against the dusty windowpane.

From the cliff, she'd walked and run eight miles through grass and scrub and climbed through woodlands strung with vines; there, little monkeys skittered on the limbs of trees with overlapping leaves that blocked the heat and light.

When the forest opened up, she'd seen a narrow road below her, curling in a double bend then gathered in the grip of interlocking slopes.

She began to sweat profusely as she left the cooler, denser woods behind and picked her way through lighter woods with smaller, thinner trees that came advancing from the road. She took the road, which she didn't realise was the very one that ran in other places on the coast, and came upon an Indian reservation.

The Indians were *caribes*; not *madrasitos*, the local name for workers who were brought from India in the 1800s to replace the slaves. The *caribes* were the remnants of the people who'd seen Columbus when he stumbled on their shore, who'd fought the Spanish for a hundred years. But like most Carlitos, they were now impure.

Apart from a tin sign hammered to a shoulder-level post, nothing marked the reservation as important or unique. It was like any other village – a little road that cut a little shop in two; little lanes that led to little huts and little fields; little ribby dogs and little naked children; women by the road selling things nobody wanted, and the dominating mass of old Diablo, the volcano that had rumbled forty years before, rising high above the other peaks.

The *caribes* were so small that at first Estrella thought that all of them were children. She found herself staring at their flat cheeks and straight hair, which most of them cut bluntly, while they looked at her with wonder and suspicion through eyes so dark and tiny that at times she thought they were closed.

She went inside a bar – a dim square in coral pink with a zinc roof stretching past the door to shade a porch supported by unshaven posts; there, a pair of women sat on stools surrounded by displays of woven objects. One wore a bonnet and the other jazzed a yellow cowboy hat, and when the tall *negrita* passed to go inside the bar, they turned around to look.

"Excuse me, what it have to eat?" Estrella asked across the counter. Two men were drinking and the barmaid looked as if she hadn't fully got over a debilitating sleep.

"It have 'possum and iguana. Fry and stew."

"No. I ain't feeling that today," she said politely, as a grimace flashed across her face.

One of the men who'd been drinking pushed a plate of bones with knots of meat on them towards her.

"It have some chicken too."

"Yes, please. I would rather take a plate o' that."

She took a table by the door so she could look outside, and the barmaid brought the food.

"This is chicken?" she asked after sniffing it. "It smell kind o' different to me."

As soon as she'd said this she remembered there was another kind of chicken here – a giant frog that lived in mountain forests and whose hind legs had the shape and juicy texture of a duck.

But you pay you money already, she thought. So you might as well eat it. Is not as if you have money to waste. You ain't eat from

16

this morning. If you eat it and pretend is something else, like octopus, then you stomach would be full. And Seville must be at least a hour or two by bus, so you should really eat. But what if this thing make you vomit? You can't look for work if you sick.

"If you don't want it, I can eat it," said the drunk from his position at the bar.

"Gimme thirty pence for it."

He wobbled off his stool.

"What? You trying to make a profit?"

"Is fifty pence I pay for it. You saving twenty pence. Is almost half price." She tossed her head towards the barmaid. "It cheaper than you would get it from she. And apart from a little piece I break off, you can't really say I even touch it. Is almost brand new."

"Well, she's my wife," the drunkard said. "And I'm the owner o' the bar. So if I want some more, I can just take it."

The woman and the other drunk began to laugh. Estrella went outside and asked the woman in the bonnet for directions to the bus. With a wrinkled thumb she pointed to the shop across the street, where a man wearing shoes was standing with a suitcase in his hand.

"What kind o' food they have over there?" Estrella asked.

"Chicken. Nice, nice chicken from right up in them hills."

"Oh."

From the reservation, the bus descended through the empty wooded hills, then moved along the coast. Before, in a landscape that was strange, the girl had felt a sense of turgid peace, but here, moving through landscapes that were familiar in some ways – she'd glimpsed them by boat – she felt a need to double-check her orientation, to challenge her understanding of ideas she'd accepted all her life.

Whole villages existed where she'd only seen the steeple of a church. The gaps between some hills were larger than she'd known. Half a mile from where she lived there was a district with a school. Buses rode higher than a boat, and when you were inside them you couldn't see the wheels.

She kept her sense of orientation by relating everything she saw to an imagined bearing on the sea. It was as if she had another, greater self out there, allowing her to see her journey from a seagull's point of view.

But when the driver turned into the northern hills to cross the island, ten miles before the rough Atlantic coast would taper to a neck and turn to swell again into the body of an avocado on the calm Caribbean shore, Estrella Thompson – miles from home – began to lose her sense of place, and tears began to trickle from her eyes.

Where I going? she thought. To who? To do what? All my relatives in country. What I going to do?

As the old bus laboured up and down the steep volcanic slopes, which were planted thickly with bananas, Estrella felt a knot of hunger harden into bone.

"What time we reaching town?" she asked across the aisle. The man who'd been waiting for the bus in shoes looked upward from his paper, which he gripped as if its pages were a thief's lapels.

"This bus isn't going to town," he said. "You wouldn't get another bus directly into town until the morning, I don't think. This one going down Speyside and turn back."

Seen from the bus, which beetled downward, Speyside was a floral accent in a plaid of greens, an embroidered rose of wood and brick in low relief against a quilt of sugarcane.

The fields were separated by a grid of roads, along which mule trains pulling wooden carts of purple canes went inching by like centipedes, raising puffs of pinkish dust.

All of this – the town, the fields, the carts – was contained by a corolla, a serrated crown of hills that gave no vision of the coast. There was about this place the sense of something continental, the sense of being in a place where life extended to the limits of ambition, a place where there were no continuous barriers like a shore.

It was late afternoon, and the streets were waiting to be filled by workers from the factory and the fields. It was the island's second largest town, about ten times smaller than Seville, and the buildings had the modesty and grace that had replaced the Spanish flair discouraged under British rule. Unlike Seville, the streets were laid out in a grid, as would be expected in a town that had been chartered as the most important base for English soldiers on the hunt for black maroons. On Estrella, the empty streets conferred an eerie feeling. She'd never seen a quiet town before.

When the driver parked the bus beside the market, the hungry girl got off. Her mind was like a fist of dice, a dark and clammy place where thoughts and choices tumbled. Decisions came. Decisions went. None of them were firm.

With her basket on her head to hide her face, she made a scouting trip along the cobbled streets that formed a square around the market, throwing furtive glances through the fence.

The old fence was brick to the height of her knees, then rose in a stockade of iron stakes above her head. Where the stakes were anchored in the brick there was a ledge where groups of people sat to watch the day, leaning forward with their elbows on their knees, the pose of age and unemployment.

It was a smaller market than the one beside the harbour in Seville, she saw. Smaller. More subdued. But like the one where she'd worked for two-thirds of her life, it was covered – but not in any fancy way – by a shingled roof supported with cast-iron beams. But unlike her market, this one didn't spill its banks and flood the streets. Also, things like pots and pans and nails were sold here. In Seville, these things were sold in shops.

But what struck her most was that the people in the market, like the people in the town, were mainly *madrasitos*. In her life she'd only seen a few.

She found them strange and fascinating, and through the iron fence she looked at them like they were creatures in a zoo. There were different types, she saw. One type wore turbans, and another wore what looked to her like small, inverted bowls of cloth. She observed intently that the *madrasitos* bought and sold according to their type. Nearly half the men wore clothes that she'd describe as "normal"; but all the women dressed in brightly coloured silk, and unlike *negritas*, seemed to live in awe of men.

Estrella sat against the ledge. On either side of her small groups of *madrasitos* roosted. They were speaking in a language that she didn't understand, and eating something with an odour that disturbed her nose.

Across the narrow street, above a white imposing fence, she saw a high extended roof with missing shingles. From behind the heavy wooden gate there came the sound of voices, buzzing saws ... the bangs and scrapes of lumber being moved.

Down the lane, a long cart filled with timbers rumbled round a bend. The cart was drawn by oxen, heavy things whose skins recalled the grubby whiteness of a butcher's coat. The beasts alone – without the cart – were almost wide enough to block the way.

Behind the cart there came a band of little children shorter than the wheels. They were brown and thin and spread across the road. From feet to ankle they were covered in the pinkish dust.

When the tall green gate was opened, Estrella looked inside the rutted yard and saw gangs of sweating men aligned on either side of heavy logs like ants about to move a turkey bone.

As he turned into the lumberyard, the driver uttered something that Estrella didn't grasp, and the men on either side of her began to laugh. The laughter spread among the children, and being the only one who didn't get the joke, she decided she'd leave.

Them people is not my people, she reflected, as she sucked her teeth and crossed her arms and walked away. They could say anything 'bout me right in front o' my face and I wouldn't even know. Plus, I ain't trust what they eating. And people who like to talk things so you don't understand, them is the kind o' people that does like to thief.

On returning to the entrance, where she'd got off the bus, she eased up on the ledge again, annoyed and apprehensive now, and gazed out on the empty street, trying to bring some order to her thoughts.

Down the sidewalk, there were women hawking trays of homemade sweets. But so great was her annoyance that she told herself that *madrasitos* sold a kind of candy that *negritas* wouldn't like.

Across the street, a bull whose shape and colour matched a rusty engine block began to bellow at the entrance of a bar. As she thought of what to do, a man, who from his looks was only partly *madrasito*, lurched out through the swinging doors and slumped against the steps and sang the bull a sweet bolero. She understood the lyrics, for he was singing in *Sancoche*, and as she drifted in the story being carried by the words – a man lamenting for a girl who ran away – her mind began to float.

If it hard to live with strangers on a little island, what it going be like when time come to live in Europe? she thought. I wonder if I could really cope with that? But it shouldn't be so hard. It only have white people in them places. And I never have no trouble with white people yet.

In her mind she saw herself in Paris. Although she'd seen pictures of the city in the *Star*, she was unable to imagine it the way it was – a grey metropolis of stone. In her mind she saw it as a vast agglomeration of the kinds of buildings that she knew, like the nicer ones she'd seen while riding into town – wooden with glass windows framed by shutters set with mini louvres, verandas framed with latticework and bougainvillea frothing over decorative railings, and shingled roofs with peaks like hills. A few would have upper floors, and those that did, especially the shops, would have their stairs outside, beneath a roof of painted zinc. It was as if her mind had an accent, and her thoughts came out of her with fresh interpretations like the patois-twisted lyrics of a European song.

After she'd thought of Paris for a very long time, she composed herself and asked a passer-by about the schedule of the bus that went to town. Like her, he was a young *negrito*. He wore a denim cap with a low brim.

"Not till 6 o'clock," he said, with what she thought of as a useless grin. "London say that petrol short, so the buses get cut back. You ain't notice you ain't see any cars?"

"I ain't see any people with sense either. What London saying 'bout that?"

"Why you so cantankerous?"

"Mind you business. If I have to reach town before that, what is there for me to do?"

He shrugged and put a fist against his chin and tapped his nose.

"You could go by the main road and beg a ride. But you ain't going get no ride right now. You have to wait until they blow the whistle over there by Royal Standard and them big trucks taking people up the hill."

"And how I would get to town from there?" she asked him, drumming her heels against the wall.

He shrugged.

"Beg another ride ... or walk ... or take the same bus you would take if you waited here till 6."

"But it ain't have other buses that ain't stop here that go to town? It have one you could take from the *caribes* straight to town they say. I take one from there that bring me here this afternoon. But is the wrong one I did take."

"I only know the bus that come there," the boy replied. "Them other buses that go other places I ain't really business with them."

Live in a place and don't know a blasted thing, she thought, as she watched him walk away. Damn head tough like concrete. Not even water can soak it, much less learning. That's why I can't live here. That's why I have to leave. Nobody ain't care to know 'bout nothing. All they care to know 'bout is their self.

In the central square, located in the nest of streets behind the bar, the town clock began to chime, and Estrella felt a lightness in her head. Along her spinal cord there ran a soft reverberation, a rising force that made her feel as if her body were the tower of the clock.

It was the force of recollection. She'd been here once before. She was four ... or five ... and she'd come with Big Tuck and her grandmother. They were visiting Big Tuck's younger brother, a chubby man who liked to laugh. He was kind, she remembered ... and when they were ready to leave he'd given her a tin whistle and a piece of boiled corn.

And as she sat there feeling stranded, she thought: That man ain't know 'bout a thing that happen with me and Big Tuck. And seeing that he's a nice man, I could tell him that Big Tuck send me for a borrows, that since the fish not coming, times hard. And who knows? He might give it to me. If I tell him they turn me out, he going take their side for sure, for blood is blood and Big Tuck ain't my blood. But first I have to find him. I know the last name and I know the pet name, but I ain't know the first name. But I ain't bound to know the first name to find him, because everybody know each other by their pet name in this place, just like my

23

friends know me as Pepper, 'cause when I cuss, my words is very hot. But lemme watch these *madrasitos*, yes. I heard they could thief milk out you coffee, and is only when you drink it you would know.

She reached to hold her basket as she jumped down off the ledge and found to her surprise that it was gone.

IV.

"Thief! Thief!"

The little naked madman dropped the mop and dashed off through the market with her basket on his shoulder, pumping with his only arm. The other one was amputated at the elbow, and he held it at the ready like a club.

He was a knobbly *yam masala*, a mix of black and Indian bloods, with ribs like an accordion and a fibrous beard that swept across his chest like a broom.

"Thief! Thief! You goddamn thief!"

The group of children who'd been following the lumber cart appeared and chanted: "Run, professor, run!"

Estrella hopped up on the ledge and hooked her toes between the staves and climbed. It was a gut reaction. She was right beside the gate.

The staves were topped with ornamental arrows made of brass, and they were sharp enough to gore her if she slipped. At the top, before the final leap, she glanced away from the madman to check her hands, but when she looked again he was gone.

Landing on her toes inside the market, she fell into a crouch and ran with doubled fists along the cobbles from the heat into the coolness of the shade.

"You see a naked fellow running with my things?" Estrella shouted as she sprinted through the aisles. They were lined with makeshift counters piled with multicoloured fruit and lumpy tubers. While speaking, she made sweeping glances like a spraying Tommy gun.

When no one answered, and she heard the way the shoppers laughed, and saw the way the vendors shook their heads, she realised that she wasn't strictly speaking what you'd call a victim; instead, she was the object of a local joke. And as she stood there with her hands against her hips she guessed they'd been communicating with each other using signs and gestures, giggling as they waited for the drama to unfold.

They think they have me going, Estrella thought. They think I ain't know what's going on. They ain't know I sell in market too. I do this to people before – laugh and carry on like I ain't see nothing. Is only sport. Is only sport. Calm yourself, Pepper. Is only sport. And if you get vex they going laugh even more. Calm yourself, Pepper. I know is wasting time. But calm yourself. You ain't know these people. And this ain't you place. You getting vex. But calm yourself. Make a sport of it. Don't take it on.

"What is *your* name?" she asked a butcher, who was smiling broadly with two rows of perfect teeth.

"They call me Asif," he said, his machete pausing then descending in a chop against a shank of beef.

"Asif," she said sweetly, "you see where the fellow with my basket gone? Tell me and I catch him for you."

"Catch him for *me*?" the butcher said, with mischief. "He ain't have nothing for me. He have something for you?"

"He might."

He leaned across the shank, which was lying on the counter, and quickly looked Estrella up and down.

"So you might have something for me too?"

"If you see anything you could use," she told him in a flirty voice that made him blush, "then tell me. Maybe we could talk."

Charmed, he cupped his mouth and shouted so everyone could hear: "If anybody find a basket in this market, please let this young lady know, because it look as if it might have been misplaced."

He said it in a language that she didn't understand and she tried to read the message in the lines above his brow.

"Is what you tell them?" she asked him in *Sancoche*, as she heard what sounded like the thing he'd said relayed from stall to stall.

"I tell them not to help the professor to hide."

"*Professor?* That's a name?"

"That's what we call him."

She said the word inside her head. She liked the sound of it. "So what that really mean?"

"I ain't exactly sure myself. But is a thing they call a man of great knowledge. And that is what he is, in truth. Don't matter how you see him there. He is a bright fellow. One o' the brightest you will ever meet. Sometimes he will straighten out and you will see him here in the market dress nicely in his shirt and trousers and a shine-up shoes. And if he come here three or four days straight like that, people will come and ask him for advice – to read letters and write letters and things like that. Because as simple as you see him now, that man went away to study doctor. And he pass all the white man exam and was supposed to come back home. But then he make a bad, bad choice. Instead o' coming home, he say he want to stay a little longer. Why? To specialise. Now, some people say is pride cause him to fall. And I agree. Because when a little man get opportunity to reach far, he must be grateful and know when he suppose to stop. But who knows? He must be see them white boys specialising and say he must reach there too. But puss and dog ain't have the same luck. A man must know when to satisfy. He couldn't satisfy. He go on and on till he burn out his brain. And it ain't lie or joke I telling you. Is my brother."

Estrella glanced across her shoulder out of instinct, looking for proof in other eyes. Was he telling her the truth? In the stall beside him, another butcher peered at her and raised his brows.

"You have to watch how you approach him," warned Asif. "He don't mean no harm, but is a mad fellow after all. But mark me – if he catch you with the nub, is like somebody beat you with a pickaxe stick."

On knees and elbows now, Estrella made her way along the aisle. Although she was in many ways mature, she was still an adolescent, young enough to make decisions on a dare. Through her dress, which had begun to cling with perspiration, the butchers watched her body shifting shape, marvelling at the way her muscles bunched then breathed into a slither, the rhythmic crest and falling of her curves.

At the end of the aisle, she slipped beneath the burlap skirting of an empty stall and scouted up and down the broader corridor that striped the selling floor in two.

Her position made her think about the stories she'd heard from men who'd hunted savage boars along the high volcanic slopes. The boars were most dangerous when cornered. So stealth – not bravery – was the best approach.

Which is why I like to fish, she thought. With fish you always have the upper hand. If he going to overpower you, you let him go.

She was shocked by this admission. Her chin was pressing on her folded arms, and she turned her head so that her arms were flat against her face. What did it mean that all her thoughts of fishing hadn't frozen into hate?

You have to harden your heart, she told herself. Otherwise, you might go back. And things ain't looking too bright. A day ain't pass and look at you. Flat on you face. Bamboozled by a fellow who ain't have all his brain. People taking you for joke. If you know what you was doing, you would reach Seville already. But you ain't really know what you doing. You ain't have no blasted use. When you see that man come out the sea, you shoulda run and shut you mouth.

28

Her mind began to squall with all the things that had occurred because she'd spoken to the diver. Thoughts leaped up and disappeared like waves. Trying to explain herself to Big Tuck and her grandmother. Dreaming of escape at night. Scaling fish alone. Sleeping in the old canoe. Hearing people whispering. The cliff. The bus. The reservation. Her own grandmother asking her to leave. And what was her grandmother thinking now? And what had she been thinking then? Did she really think she'd cursed the fish?

You can't curse anything, Estrella thought. Only God and the *orishas* could do that. Everybody know that. If is one thing I sure of, is that. Maybe all o' this is punishment. 'Cause I was thinking like a liar and a thief and then – *bam!* – my basket gone. I ain't even know if what I think I might remember is true. As I think about it now, I ain't even sure if Big Tuck even have a younger brother in this place, or if this is even the place where I come that time. I was only four or five. But what happen already happen. If I lose that basket I lose everything except my money and my knife. My only toy. My best books. My blanket. My only change o' clothes. If I lose them things what I going do? 'Cause I can't go back. Knowing them, they wouldn't even take me. And to go back to let them put me out again would be a disgrace.

As she often did when she found herself in situations where she'd lost control, Estrella felt the absence of her mother.

Her name was Edwina. Estrella didn't know that she'd died.

What she look like? How old she be? What kind o' work she do? What kind o' mood she have? Quiet ... bossy ... jokey ... tough? She have a husband? Other children? Or is me alone?

Whenever she'd asked these questions, her grandmother would answer with evasion or a grunt. Some things were not discussed.

Like why she move from Trinidad to Cuba. Or if she had a trade when she was young. Or why she move from Cuba to San Carlos. Or who her husband was before she meet Big Tuck.

The absence of her mother, in and of itself, didn't make Estrella feel alone. Relations in the cove were so close. All children more or less belonged to all adults – which didn't mean they were bathed in love. They were supervised and overseen, disciplined and watched, but when it came to close attention, children were ignored. They had no special place. There was no myth of them as warm, big-hearted beings. They were simply small adults. They worked.

The communal role of parents was encouraged by the fact that certain kinds of incest were allowed. It wasn't uncommon for cousins or half-siblings to marry, mate – or even fall in love. And marriage was a matter of the common law.

If you cooked a man's food and washed his clothes, and if he slept with you and didn't try to leave in secret in the morning, and this went on for what was understood to be awhile, then you were known as man and wife.

This idea also ruled the ownership of land. If you found a beach and built a shack on it, and went to sea from it, and fixed your nets on it, and beached your boat on it, there was a common understanding that the beach belonged to you.

However, people didn't move, didn't branch away to live alone – for in the deepest part of their collective understanding, they could only see themselves as part of something vaguely known as "one".

To be a fragment or a fraction was the greatest fear. So exile was the harshest form of retribution – the punishment reserved for those whose thoughts and actions undermined the fundamental meaning of their lives.

When she'd thought of all these things, Estrella rolled away from underneath the skirting and began to move with purpose down the aisles. Her steps were heavy. From a distance, even with the sound of other voices, you could hear the thudding of her heels against the floor.

Her face was blank, but tight with concentration, like a gambler who's taken full account of what he's lost and what he's going to lose unless he sinks this ball or draws this card; who can't quit, because quitting means it's over; who can't just walk away, because walking is what losers do.

When you lose like that it's not the same as losing fair and square. Losing fair and square will sharpen you, will give you edge, will make you the kind of person who'll win again. But when you walk away you don't just lose the game, you lose a little bit of nerve; and when that starts to happen, then your gambling days are done; they'll look at you and call your bluff and you'll look at them and worry, then you'll always lose; and winning is for winners, and losing isn't nice.

As she walked, Estrella slipped a hand into the pocket with the blade.

"Where's the fellow with my things?" she asked Asif when she'd covered all the aisles.

"I have no idea," he said with a laugh. "When I see you lying down I think you gone to cry."

She put her hands on the counter, slowly but with force, and glared at him from way beneath her brows.

"I look like a person that cry easy?"

"I ain't say nothing like that."

"Because you see I black you think I fool?"

"I never say you was no fool," he said carefully.

"Well, you talking the way I talk to idiot people."

Her glare began to affect him, and he raised his hands to shoulder height and told her, "Look, I ain't want no fuss with you. Better you just go you way."

"Well, I ain't want none either," she answered, in a louder voice. "I just want my things. I just want to go." She spoke quietly again. "I asking you another time, sir. You see the fellow with my things?"

"It ain't necessary to come to this," he told her in a voice that made aggressive use of overdone restraint. "Just wait a little while and don't make no fuss and everything will be okay. If you make a fuss, things mightn't go the way you want them. And I want things to work for you. Nobody here ain't thief."

"You ain't really know who you playing with," she answered, backing off. She spread her arms and spun around. "I will break up this place until somebody talk to me." She leaned down on his counter now as people shuffled down the aisle. "It ain't funny. It ain't funny at all. You ain't know where I coming from or where I going. You ain't know me from Adam. You ain't know me at all. You ain't know what I will do." She sprung back and straightened up and pointed now. "I will mash up everything in this goddamn place until I get my things, Asif. You hear me? Not because you see me black so. I ain't no simpleton. I ain't have no mother supervising me. I ain't no goddamn child."

From a nearby stall, Estrella grabbed a hairy coconut and smashed it on the floor. The juice erupted in a silver fizz. A woman shrieked as jagged fragments zoomed.

"Take time," said Asif. "Take time."

"I can't take what I ain't have. I want to go 'bout my business, and here you is interfering with my life. I laugh already. I give you that, Asif. I give that to all o' you. And I ain't going laugh no more. I ain't come here to turn into nobody clown. I give you entertainment. I give you a show. So, coolie man, gimme my damn things now."

"Who she calling, *coolie*?" someone shouted over mutterings in a language that Estrella didn't understand. "What? She want somebody cut her ass?"

"I will mash somebody skull," Estrella answered. Her neck was taut. She felt she'd break it if she turned to look. "You watching me? You follow? Just like how you see that coconut? I'll mash a skull like that. You don't know where I coming from and you don't know where I going. Don't push me no more."

She sensed someone approaching from behind and turned around to see a hefty woman in a sari stealing sideward down the aisle.

"If you trouble one, you trouble all," the woman warned. "You can't come here and break up people things like this and think you could just go."

"Same way you shouldn't let you people take my things and don't say nothing. So is even. One for one."

As Estrella grabbed another coconut, a butcher with a turban rushed her from the side, and she took his arm and drew her knife and turned him off her ass.

"Stop it," said Asif after his *compadre*'s head and back collided with the floor. "Everybody stop."

The groaning man was barely moving. But they saw no sign of blood.

When Estrella backed away, aware now of the danger to her life, Asif came from behind his counter with her basket in his hand. One leg was withered, and he had a limp that made him waddle like a seal.

"Take it and go," he said. "Take it and go. It ain't have to come to this. Just take you things and go."

"Where you get it from?" she asked him as her heart began to pound. Another person lunged towards her. Asif leaned in and used his arms and chest to block the blow.

"Spare you life," he told Estrella. He gave a sign and two men hauled off the one who'd attacked her, no doubt for a smack-up down the aisle. "Listen what I say and go. Don't turn back. Run. Don't walk. That man you throw down is the most ignorant man I ever see. And the fellow I had to rough up was his son. Listen what I tell you. Go! Pick up you life in you hand and go! And learn to take a joke!"

V.

Estrella ran out of the market and stampeded past the rusty bull that had been sung to sleep outside the bar.

Knees pumping almost navel high, she took a bend that led her through an alleyway with doors that opened straight into the street, and swerved around a group of men in undershirts who'd set up stools around a table on the cobbles for their game of dominoes.

Emerging from the alleyway, she squinted as she headed down a path that led her past the finger-pointing tower of the spired clock, and slanted in a wheeling semicircle round a little park where children played a game of cricket with a two-by-four, then veered off by the courthouse with its large, imposing columns and its curving marble stairs and took the road by which the bus had brought her into town.

Raised with clannish people, she knew of all that could occur. So although she didn't hear the sound of feet behind her, or get the sense that all the people who were laughing as she ran were going to gather in a mob, she sprinted, as she'd later tell her children, "like I heard a rumour that a rich old auntie came to visit from abroad".

As she came upon the steep ascent, she cursed and tensed her middle, hunching forward, giving greater power to her legs, which laboured with the challenge of the slope; and for half a mile she grunted onward till the band of muscles in her middle, which resembled little squares, began to soften like a chocolate bar.

Tired and hungry, she began to walk. They ain't coming, she thought, and put her hands against her hips. She glanced across her shoulder down the steeply rising road, which disappeared around a bend into the bush.

They have better things to do, she told herself. But a coward man keep sound bones, as them old people say. I ain't able for anybody to gimme a chop or a cuff right now. But anyways, is a good thing it happen, in a way, 'cause you had to get out o' that damn place. You was only loitering and wasting time when you have important things to do. You have to get to town. And town way, way far away. And you have to get there before night come. 'Cause by 7:30 all them big stores going be closed. And that is the first place you have to go – a store where they sell shoes. 'Cause ain't nobody giving any sensible job where you ain't have to wear no shoes. And you have to get a job before tomorrow. 'Cause you ain't have a soul in town.

As she spiralled up the lonely road Estrella fantasised about her coming life, and saw an older version of herself creating stares and whispers of excitement when her driver brought her to Salan's, the island's most elite department store – two floors, a wooden escalator, a soda fountain, and a cafeteria with a balcony that overlooked the Queens.

Smiling with a puckered mouth as if she held a secret, Estrella saw herself among the aisles, wearing yellow satin pumps – fancy shoes that had the bag and dress to match, her husband's black fedora as an accent on her head, and behind her, waiting, a clerk whose arms were filled with boxes, calling her "Madame".

The main cross-island road was seven miles away, and Estrella worked towards it at a slow but steady pace. From time to time, small herds of goats would trickle down the road or drip in ones and twos out of the dark encroaching woods, which at certain points would form a roof of shade.

Later, after she'd noticed that the goats were coming down the mountain in a heavy stream – groups of ten and twelve – she came upon a clump of leaning huts. To her mind they were the poorest homes she'd ever seen. They were made of cracked, ill-fitting timbers that had not been planed, and between some of the timbers there were spaces large enough to slip a hand.

The shaggy huts were built on stilts to keep them level. With their brown walls and dry roofs they looked like herds of animals reduced to skin and bone by drought. In their shadows lingered clouds of little children, their heads as round and dark as lice.

As she looked, an old *negrita* standing in the shadow of a doorway wiped her hands against her dress, which was a flour sack, and asked her with a mouth that had collapsed against its gums, "You hungry, sweetheart? You want a little something?"

And in a moment of illumination, Estrella knew that these were not the poorest homes she'd ever seen. Her people in the cove had homes like these.

Looking at the dirt she hadn't dusted from her clothes, her hands entangled in her fraying hair, feeling dust transforming into mud along her sweaty feet and shins, glancing as she passed the old *negrita*, Estrella held her basket and began to run again, her breathing dry and cracked with effort, like someone waking from nightmarish dreams.

She was at a height now where the intermittent grunts and groans of vehicles on the main cross-island road began to filter through the net of soft translucent sounds that caught and held the chirrups of the woods.

Her feet were budding with the early pain of blisters, whispered pangs that felt as if her soles were giving birth to cleats. Although the pain had not emerged completely, she began to hobble, balanced on the outer lines that marked the point at which her soles were fused against the uppers of her leather-coloured feet.

Eventually, Estrella came upon a bridge. It was old and white, with small columns at each end and parapets of stone. On approaching it, she saw a path that led into a bamboo grove and heard the sizzle of a stream. After taking minutes to decide, she headed down the path and inched her way towards the water, holding onto creaking stems to keep herself from falling, watching out for razor-pointed stumps.

It was a narrow stream, thirty yards across, and she came out of the thick, steep-sided forest onto rugged grass that grew along the wide embankment.

She sat against the edge of the embankment with her feet above the flow, and lay back in the furry hotness of the grass, the sun pressing on her like a boy who'd waited long for them to be alone.

When she'd rested for a while, she stripped and lay there thinking, her body smooth as wood without the bark, then slipped into the olive stream.

She cavorted with amphibian ease, turned on her back and stroked like a frog with her forceful legs, then twisted sharply in a shallow dive, head down, toes long, strong arms by her side, tadpoling over stones and grass along the muddy bed.

In the middle of the stream there was a scattered line of oval rocks that had been sanded by erosion to an eggy whiteness, and she played at leaping on their warm, protruding tops although the landing sometimes stung her feet.

After she'd played, she used a hunk of soap to wash her purple dress and underwear and laid them on the grass, then swam against the current to the point at which the river swung beneath an arch of overhanging trees and fell in baby steps.

She sat against the broad, flat stone that she'd felt for with her hands beneath the flow, braced her feet against two upright ones, and let the falling water pound her neck and back. Although the stream was moving slowly and the drop was from a shallow height, the water had the power of a solid force, and as it hammered her, she felt old fears dispersing and the hairs that formed her brows untwining from their knit. She closed her eyes and smiled out of her diamond face while spitting plastered hair out of her mouth.

I is the luckiest girl in the world right now, she thought. It might have people with more money and thing. But right now, as I feeling this water on me and hear them birds how they make sweet sounds, it ain't have nobody with more luck than me.

She returned downstream to bathe. With a scrap of cloth, Estrella creamed her body in a slop of suds. The whiteness of the soap against her dark complexion made it seem as if she were about to hide herself in snow.

Her waist was tightly tapered, and her breasts were little banks of mud with twigs. She had no cleavage, and standing up her bosom looked the same as when she lay down; but her hips were matriarchal and her buttocks had deep clefts, and when she sank into the stream to rinse, emerging from the slick of suds to walk towards the bank, she was the vision of a goddess coming through the clouds.

On the bank, she wrung her hair as if it were a towel and lay down on her stomach in the grass beside her dress. With her face against her folded arms she listened to the sloshing water and, above her head, the flap of lifting wings. And for the first time in her life, she experienced what it meant to have the privacy in which to read.

From her basket, which was placed beside her head, she took her only toy, a wooden doll with missing arms that she'd never named, and read the story of another girl who'd led an awful life. Her reading voice was mumbled and self-conscious, and she didn't fully understand what punctuation meant, as such she ran through periods and rear-ended sentence openings like a granny at the wheel.

When she read, she overlaid her life against the tale of Cinderella and felt a smoky joy, a kind of bluesy satisfaction, which, in *Sancoche* was called *memweh*, for which there is no good translation. In English, the closest feeling is nostalgia. But this is not enough. *Memweh* is nostalgia for a person or a thing that might have existed in another life, a vital kind of sadness experienced as a grope, like swimming upward from deep water into light and breaking through the surface only to be covered by a wave, then sinking with a glimpse of something beautiful that propels you to grope upward once again, a lament for the amnesia of the middle passage, a search for a suspected loss that only *negritos* fully understand.

How I never meet nobody like a prince? Estrella thought, caught up in the tidal cycle of *memweh*. I wonder if it have men like that in truth. It would shock them if a man like that come sweep me off my feet, I tell you. Old Tuck and my grandmother would lose their mind. That would shame them, boy. I tell you. They think I ain't going come to nothing in this life. But watch me. When I get to town and get my shoes and get a job and work and save my money and put myself together with my shoes that match my bag and my bag that match my frock, I going meet a man who going make me feel like that white lady at La Sala that day. Me and my husband, all we going do all day is write each other notes. Even when I see him face-to-face, I going slip one in his pocket so he can read it later. For no reason. Just for so.

But in nearly fifteen years on earth, she'd never seen a man who looked like her do anything that anyone considered princely, had never seen a woman of her colour being treated in a way that made her think of queens.

She'd seen *negritos* giving women what Carlitos knew as "talks", frilly conversation on a sheet of innuendo, seen fellows making women tremble with their bluff. But she'd never heard a loving word from a *negrito* if it wasn't in a song, or witnessed a *negrito* read a book, or heard about *negritos* who would do these things. Not even in a rumour or a tale.

When she thought of all of this, Estrella gave herself an explanation – like fashion, all things go in and out of style, and maybe, long ago, before her time, *negritos* used to do the kinds of things that people came to know as white. So one day, when styles had changed, they'd do these things again.

She curled up on her side, stretched out on her back, crossed her arms beneath her head, and pursed her lips as if she'd tasted something that was sweet but acidic.

Of the men she'd been with, who'd come the closest to a prince? There'd been a few, for she'd lost her hymen at the age of twelve when a game of wrestling accidentally put her and a playmate in a pose that triggered the desire to explore. With this kind of introduction, sex for her was something rugged – a game in which she liked to have the upper hand. She must win and he must lose. He must like it more than me. I ain't want to be no woman who exchange rum for man. I ain't want to be no cockaholic.

With a finger on her nipple, she began to stroke her tender parts until the air was crackled by a tiny scream.

She lay there half-smiling till her strength returned.

VI.

On the bridge, she leaned against the parapet and waited. Her purple dress was not completely dry, but she'd packed it and was wearing now her only change of clothes – a dark blue skirt and a green striped blouse, both of which were old.

With her hair down to her shoulders, her face seemed more mature; and features that had not revealed themselves before were now pronounced. She had a small nose with a low bridge that ended in a smooth, compacted mound, and nostrils that you couldn't see unless she raised her head.

Her mouth was small and oval like a circle cut in two. The upper lip was shiny, with a reddish tone, and from its corners ran an upward-slanting seam that made it look as if her mouth and cheeks were linked beneath the skin with guitar strings. The space between her nose and mouth was close, as if her lips were resting on a sheet of glass; and where the hair along her temples grew towards her brow, there was a scar, a little crescent moon, whose ridge of smoothness you could follow with your thumb.

She heard the sound of diesel engines and looked with expectation down the road, then stood up when she saw the tall, imposing grillwork of a truck.

It lurched around the bend and rumbled by so closely that she could've stretched her hand and touched it. It was filled with *madrasitos*, workers from the factory and the fields, and their limbs protruded through the gaps between the slatted sides that formed the bed like they were stalks of cane. Some sat on the cab as if it were an elephant's head. Those who found a ledge on which to hook their toes and fingers rode along the side; and she watched the driver take the curves without regard, coming close against the bush, as if the people holding on were fleas.

I ain't able for them people, thought Estrella, as the *madrasitos* called to her and waved. They run me out their town already. I ain't want to get inside no truck with them. Worst of all, they have machete. I ain't going nowhere with them. The fellow by the market said it have a bus. I prefer to wait for that. Plus is only dirty people I seeing in them trucks. And I now just bathe myself.

The trucks were coming close together in a convoy like an army in retreat, and she kept her eyes engaged by reading so she didn't have to look.

But when another thirty minutes passed and she hadn't seen the bus, and the gaps between the trucks began to lengthen to the point where she would hear one engine fading out before another grunted up the hill, she changed her mind.

VII.

The truck was crowded, but not as crowded as the ones that came before. No one clung against the side or rode the cab. But those who had seats were stacked on others like jars of pickled pork. With their backs against the cab, hats aligned in humps below the glass, some were sitting on the truck's short bed with hands around their ankles, chins against their knees, gazing at their toes. The others stood and held onto the ribbing of the missing canvas sheet.

The old blue truck groaned on. It was a Pierce-Arrow from the '20s, with an upright cab like a telephone booth and light external fenders of the type you see on motorbikes today. It was older than the other trucks, and smaller, and rode like a carriage on weak leaf springs that creaked.

With the engine under stress, they passed a scrappy settlement and turned onto the main cross-island road.

They came upon a string of solid villages with paved streets and good houses – verandas, hedges, lattice trim – a pond below the wreckage of a white great house, then for miles, on rolling land, long rows of young banana trees just planted by United Fruit. Guards rode up and down the verge on horses – some of them with guns.

From there, the road was like a lashing whip, and the old truck rose and fell along its dips and rises, flanked by humps of land in terraced cultivation – tenant farms of beans and cabbage next to ample citrus groves whose owners had new cars and concrete villas.

The truck made frequent stops, and Estrella dropped her head each time. This way she wouldn't feel compelled to wave.

Although she was grateful that they'd slapped their hands against the truck to make the driver stop, and had gripped her arm and helped her in, Estrella held the workers in contempt. They'd failed. They were dirty and poor, and wore their tattered clothes on bodies in decay.

In their company she felt as if her bath had been a waste. Above them hung a tender stink that slipped inside her body when she sighed or made a sharp intake of breath – as she did on seeing a man unearth a booger from his nose and crush it on his sleeve.

The stores would be closed when she got to Seville, which meant she'd be going to bed without a job, and waking up without a future in the morning, after sleeping who-knows-where.

"Which part you going?" somebody asked.

Without looking she replied, "I going town."

By now she was the only person standing, and was staring at the road behind her as it faded into dusk.

She felt the heat of eyes on her, and when she looked she saw a woman leaning forward to reveal the man who'd asked. He was in his twenties, with a handsome face spoiled in places by a rash, and as she peered at him Estrella wondered why he didn't hide it with a beard.

"Which part you coming from?" he asked.

The leaning woman put her elbows on her knees, and now the man looked like her bidet.

Estrella answered, "Far."

"Far like far where? Every far has a name."

"Farther than you'd want to go."

"How you know that?"

"I ain't know that. And I ain't care that you know I ain't know that. Worse, I ain't care what you want to know for."

"Suppose I have important reasons?"

"I'd say 'good for you.'"

"Well, it must be good for me. Because I want to know so I could go and see you mother and thank her. For she made a lovely girl like you."

When the laughter in the truck had died, he pointed at the woman in his lap and said, "Don't worry. Me and her ain't nothing. When she gone I'll take you."

"If you know where I want to go, you wouldn't say that."

"How you know for sure?"

"Well, you old enough. If you did want to go you'd be gone already."

"Maybe I was waiting for you."

"Some kind o' things can't cook in the same pot," she said, annoyed but also quite amused. "Some things together is poison. Like cornmeal and rum. You ever drink that?"

"No."

"Next time I see you, remind me, and I promise to make some for you."

The people in the truck began to laugh again.

"You hair pretty," he said almost shyly. "You have Indian in you?"

"No."

"You want some?"

"You're a blasted fool. You know that?"

"Stop acting like you vex. I can see you want to laugh."

"It have children just like you, you know. They fill they eye before they fill they belly. They always asking for big plate o' food and when they get it they choke."

"I never hear a truer word," a woman in a red bandanna said. She tapped Estrella on the arm and offered her a lighted cigarette.

Estrella sat on the tailgate, held onto the frame, crossed her legs, and smoked, the slow wind picking on her still-damp hair.

45

She had the nature of a gambler, and as she smoked, her lips began to clamp more tightly as she played the conversation back and forth in her mind. She felt as if she'd lost.

"Which part you want to take me to?" she asked the man directly.

"Well ..."

"Don't play jackass now. I'm interested. Tell me where you want me and you to go. Where this place is where they giving people Indian blood?" She took her deepest drag, then added, "Or is Indian baby you did say?"

As the workers chuckled, Estrella laughed and settled down to smoke again.

"Vashti, you can't have them woman laughing so," a man began to tease.

"What you want me do? Beat her?"

"No. It ain't call for that. A man like you so full o' argument should have the strength to give her back some talks."

"You right. I going take you advice. So," he started, looking at Estrella now, "you want to know where I going take you? That is what you want to know, right? Well, hear now where I going take you. Listen good and—"

"Vashti, cut the shit and talk nuh, man."

"You want to know where I going take you?" he began again. "That is what I was going tell you before this eunuch interrupted me. Well, hear now where I going take you. Listen good. I going take you to a place where you not going know yourself. Where you going see yourself and wonder if is you because you never see yourself like that before ... looking happy like you just finish eating a plate o' goat stew with white yam ... like when the goat stew finish and you make a belch and cut a fart you best friend give you back the money he borrow thirty years ago ... with *interest* ... and take you down the bar and put *your* drinks on *his* tab. But it ain't done yet. Because after you leave the bar, you go

46

to church and find that Jesus tell the pastor to forgive all them rudeness I could look at you and tell you like to do." He paused to add a dash of intrigue and excitement. "You is a bad girl. I can tell. An experienced Indian ever take the time to light a fire on you tail?"

She sucked her teeth and didn't answer.

"Eh?" he prompted.

"Sister, what you have in the basket?" someone asked her from a corner by the cab. "It have anything to eat?"

"It ain't have no food," she said, smirking in the dimming light. "It have book though. And soap. But if you look like you friend here who just tell me all this stupidness, then book and soap ain't make for you."

"Boy, the country girl have words, eh?" Vashti said.

"And you from which part?" Estrella answered. "Paris? You acting like you come from town. Man, don't try me this evening. All you make for is one thing."

The woman in the red bandanna fired: "That's to burn and throw away."

They were easing down into the flats now, where the central mountains stuttered in a taper to the Caribbean coast. Only four of them remained – three workers and Estrella, who by now knew all their names.

The naughty banter had evolved into an easy conversation, during which she'd shared with them a little of her life, and they'd shown a new regard for the *negrita* when she lit a match and grabbed a book from her basket and showed that she could read.

When the truck reached its final stop, four miles before the intersection with the coastal road, Vashti, the man who'd tried to give her talks, said, "Wait here while we see what we can do."

The workers gathered by the driver's door, and Vashti said, "Do me a favour, boss, and take her down the road?"

"She who?" came the sharp reply.

"The girl we pick up by the Sandy River Bridge. She going town."

"That's what you telling me now," the driver said impatiently. "But I ain't business with that. This ain't even my truck. Rambana drive my truck and crash it last week and now I have to drive this skeleton they dig up from the boneyard. I ain't even know if it can take them hills it have to go back home."

"It can take it, man. It can take it. Have faith. Is a old truck, but it good. Look how it carry all o' we from clear down Speyside to here."

"Vashti, you can't even drive a cow out you yard, but you want to give me advice?"

"Is far she coming from, you know, Joseph. Is not just from the bridge. Is far. From way down the Atlantic side. I ain't asking you to take her all the way. Just down to the coast road. You ain't even have to run the engine. You could just make it glide."

"Have a heart nuh, Joseph," said the woman with the red bandanna. "Have a heart. Do it, nuh. God will bless you."

The driver cleared his throat.

"I have a heart," he said. "I have a heart in truth. But I want to have a job too. So tell her get out o' my truck."

The woman in the red bandanna stepped away and looked up at the disappointed girl. "*Your* people is a funny people," she said, enraged. "They say everybody fight them, but they love to fight themselves."

As Estrella bit her lip and thought of what to say, the woman stepped up on the running board and shouted in the driver's face.

"Joseph, you is a worthless nigger man! A worthless nigger man! The child trying to reach somewhere and you is the only

48

body who could help her, and look how you going on. Down by the estate you like to talk you tripe 'bout unionise, and work together, and black and Indian must help each other. And here it is now, you wouldn't even try to help you own kind. We is Indian and we care more than you. You is a disgrace to you blasted race. You is a damn disgrace. Listen – the next time you see me, don't tell me nothing 'bout Marcus Garvey and all them tripe. Just don't tell me nothing. As a matter o' fact, don't even drive me in you blasted truck again. If you see me in you way and you driving you truck, Joseph, just run over me to *rass*. Just run right over my head. And run over me from behind, because I ain't want see you blasted ugly face no more."

With this she tramped away.

"In '35 when we strike," the driver answered, his voice low but poised to grow into a bulging force, "I take bullet in my ass and baton in my head for ungrateful *rasses* like you. Damn coolie! You is a blight on the black man. You is a lice. They bring you here so we couldn't get we proper pay when free paper come, 'cause the white man know *your* kind would work for rum and a bowl o' curry rice. But when I call the strike, you wouldn't stand with me. That's why we don't have any blasted union in San Carlos today, and Rawle could pay we what he want to pay we. Because o' folks like you. Everybody in the West Indies striking those times ... St Kitts, Jamaica, St Vincent, St Lucia ... and all o' them get their union from that, except we. Why? Because o' people like you. That's why we ain't have nothing in this country." He paused to catch his breath. "I is a old man, trying to live out my days. And you want to pressure me to prove myself to you? To bow down to you? To do what you want me to do just because you say so? Why I should follow you? You name Gandhi?"

I ain't want no *bangarang* because o' me, Estrella thought. Lemme just take my things and go.

"Oyi," she called to Vashti. "Let him go. His conscience going jam him tonight." She came down from the truck and stood beside the disfigured man.

He put his hand on her head and mumbled, "Sorry."

"It ain't nothing to sorry 'bout," she said with disappointment. "It ain't nothing to sorry 'bout at all. I come farther than a lot o' people think I could go. But thank you anyway."

"You know, as long as we talking I ain't know you name."

"Listen it good."

She told him with her lips against his ear. He tapped her on the shoulder with a disenchanted look on his disfigured face and said, "Don't make anything happen to you, you hear?" and walked into the bush towards a bobbling light.

"Is not my fault," the driver said when he and Estrella were left alone. "If it was up to me, I would take you. But I ain't even think it have enough petrol in this thing. And if it stop with me out here on the road, how anybody going to know? Plus my wife and children waiting at home."

Estrella placed her back against the door, her face away from him. "Is not me you have to tell," she said as she thought of what to do. "I ain't ask you for a thing. Is they ask you. I ain't ask them to ask you. Is them is you friend. Is them you let down. It ain't me." She slammed her hands against the door and walked away. "So don't say a goddamn thing to me."

"I ain't supposed to do this," said the driver, leaning from the cab. "If they find me out, is *rass*."

She turned around with a hand across her brow, her body silvered by the high beams, heard his work boots crunching down the grade, then saw his back-lit shadow slowly coming into view.

When he was beside her, she saw that he was stocky, and wore glasses on a peanut-coloured face. His silver hair receded sharply, and he'd shaved his moustache in a pencil line.

"Let me take the basket. Come."

She climbed into the cab. When they were coasting down the road she asked him, "Who's Mr Rawle?"

The windshield had a set of hinges where it met the roof. He'd opened it so that it formed an awning, and the wind was blowing straight against her face.

"On this island," he began, "it have three families that count. It have Rawle. It have Campbell. It have Salan. Rawle and Campbell is like one because o' marriage. And soon it going be Rawle alone since Salan young daughter married Rawle big boy. Rawle own sugar on this island. Rawle own cattle on this island. Rawle own coconuts. And although he get a blow with the coconut blight, and although he had to sell off most o' the estates so that he only have this Speyside now, and although nobody buying beef now because o' the war, Rawle is still the sheriff in this town. You see Salan?" He glanced at her to see if she was listening. "He's coming up fast. And I like him more, because he is a man that start out poor, and he deal with people with manners. But you have to watch him, 'cause them Jews and Lebanese is tricky like *rass*." He tapped her shoulder. "I watching this scene long time, you know. I know what's going on. I bet you a thousand pounds that before I dead Salan going richer than Rawle. I don't know exactly how. But I know it going happen. Lemme show you how the man full o' tricks. Just when the war break out and Rawle get lick with the coconut blight, Salan go to Rawle and said, 'Lemme take some swampland off you hands.' Well, Rawle like a fool go and sell him. Well, guess what? Before you know it, the Americans leasing this land from Salan to make a airbase. Now why would anybody build a airbase on a swamp? Because they need plenty land that is flat near the sea, and this place is only mountains. So the Americans use their big machine

51

and dig down a hill and use that dirt to fill up a swamp. But guess whose hill? Salan. And guess what again? Salan want to flatten that hill long, long time, but he couldn't find a way to do it cheap. And guess whose land they dump?"

"Salan," she said distractedly, while thinking, I hear he also sell the nicest shoes.

"You're a brains. You hear what I telling you?" He beat his hands against the steering wheel. "You *get* what I saying. You *understand* my point. So, the Americans spend their money to fill up this land with soil, and then the next thing you know they not building no base again. And the next thing after that you hear is that Salan take that swampland and planting acres and acres o' cane. Miles and miles o' cane. You see how the man smart?"

"He should open a school."

"But it ain't book smart that man have," the driver emphasised. "It ain't book smart at all. That man have common sense because he's a common man. And that is why I like him. He's a common man. Rawle act too high and mighty, like his shit come from Nova Scotia in a tin like sardine. And the only thing that is making him ride high right now is that Royal Standard Rum. That is the best rum it have in the world. I hear people talking 'bout Bacardi and Appleton and Havana Club like them rum is anything to talk 'bout. Listen to what I saying tonight. I take them rum and wash my glass before I tip the best. And is one place grow the cane for that rum and that is Speyside. That's where grow the finest cane. And that's why they build that factory there in that bowl that so hard to get to. You lose the quality if you make that rum from them fields it have near the sea. And that is why it burn me when them lice-head coolie never stand by me when we make that strike in '35. Because if it had union in this country, we could boil down Rawle and all them *rasses* till they reach the bottom o' the pot. A lot o' people vex that the

Americans taking over ... talking all kind o' *rass* 'bout how they ain't trust United Fruit. But in a sense I glad. One man beating my ass all my life. I say let another man come and lick me and see how it sweet."

"You would be vex if I tell you I ain't feel like to talk?" Estrella asked him dryly.

"If I would *mind*?" he asked, offended. "If I would *mind*? Of course I would blasted mind. I giving you a blasted ride ... you better talk to me. Them people I work with ain't talk to me. They think I talk too much. And some say I must be a spy because how I could cuss Mr Rawle so much and he ain't fire me yet. But I ain't stupid. I ain't cuss the man to him face. I cuss him to his back. I old now. I do my time. This job to drive this truck here is the only thing I have name pension. When I was cutting and leaf was slicing up my flesh was a long, long time ago. When I born it still had slaves in Cuba. Brazil too. A lot o' people ain't know those things. But they ain't read books, you see. They ain't read books. So they ain't know what's going on."

"I like to read," she said, interested now.

"For true?"

"Yes. I like it more than anything it have in the world."

"So how you can read but you talk like you ain't go to school?" he asked, amazed.

"I can speak English," she said, switching from *Sancoche*. "But I have never been to school. I taught myself and I received a little help from a Chinese girl whose father owns a shop."

"You are a prize," he said, pulling over. "A real, fantastic prize. What is you name?"

"Why you want to know?" she asked defensively.

"So I could present you with a proper compliment."

She leaned over her basket, which she carried in her lap.

"I ain't want nobody to tie up my head right now," she said, reverting to *Sancoche*. "I ain't want nobody compliment me or

53

anything like that 'cause that is only talks. I going 'bout my business, you see me here. And that is all I want to do."

When they'd begun to coast again, he asked, "Why you going to town so late?"

"I have business down there."

"When I leave you off," he asked with genuine concern, "how you going to reach?"

"I ain't know for sure."

"Girl, it going be real hard to get a vehicle driving that way, you know. Unless is a emergency, you shouldn't try to go."

"Is a emergency in truth for me. I sick. I real sick. I real sick o' this place."

She turned so that her back was pressing on the door and placed a thigh against his seat. "Mister, you would never imagine what happen to me."

"Tell me."

But how I could trust a man who only cuss his boss behind his back? she thought. A man like that is a two-face man. You suppose to say what you feel. 'Cause talk is what make a man greater than a beast. And when you say behind a man what you want to say to his face you showing him something. You showing him that he's a man and you is some kind o' mule for him to ride, or some kind o' dog for him to kick around. And people who take so much kick and ride, they mind weak. And they will talk you business when the pressure start to come. That's exactly what happen to me. My own friends who was there when that man come out the waves tell lie and spread rumour 'pon me. They 'fraid o' what come out their parents' mouth.

"Let it rest," she told the driver. "Let it rest. But something happen to me that make me sick down to my soul."

In his head he said, *This subject needs a change.*

"I hear that fire burning down in Black Well," he said.

"Which part is that?" she asked.

"On the way to town."

"I never hear 'bout no place name so. Which part is that? And when you say burning, what kind o' burning you mean?"

"I ain't really know. A man tell me today that they was burning down there again. You ain't know which part Black Well is?"

She shook her head and made a grunt.

"That is where Salan get the Yankee them to fill up the swamp so he could plant the cane. The same place we old people call New Lagos is the same place name Black Well now. When I was a young man a Yankee priest name Father Eddie ... Eddie Blackwell was his name ... use to do some things out there. Have woman and all, I hear. Maybe that's why they call it so. But still, it have some o' the blackest nigger man you ever see out there. So maybe that's why they call it so."

"You mean where it have some houses in the water on the poles?" she asked. "And sometimes out there you could catch manatee?"

"Same one."

"Yes. I know out there."

After they'd driven for a mile in silence, which Estrella utilised to prep her mind to walk, the driver took a hand from off the wheel.

Looking at the girl, her tousled hair, her diamond face, her upper lip, which was encroaching on her nose, he began to rub the leather knob that crowned the long gear stick that slanted from the floor.

I ain't able for this *rass*, Estrella thought. I ain't able for this *rass* right now. But you almost there. It can't turn into nothing big. If he try to force you then it have to be a fight.

"You have a boyfriend?" he began.

"I might," she said flatly.

"You do or you don't?"

"Why you want to know?"

"I have a son," he said nobly. "A nice boy. The youngest one. Nineteen years old with a good trade. He's a mechanic down at Royal Standard. He's a man can fix anything that break. But is only Indian girls he like. That woman in the red bandanna who just cuss me off, she carrying bad feelings for me. Why? It have a rumour that my son fooling with her girl. But that ain't true. My son have taste. My son know better than that. My son is a educated boy. Can read and write. And her daughter would see her name on a envelope with money and use it to wipe her ass. By the way, how old you be?"

"Old enough," she said, smiling.

"I ain't want none o' them town girls for my son. Them girls have too much guile. He need a nice country girl with ambition. A girl who could read and write." He raised his hand to make the point. "And she must be pretty too. What man want a bright, ambitious monkey in the bed?"

Estrella laughed.

"I ain't making joke," he said. "Is a serious thing. Just like no woman ain't have no use for no fat man. No man ain't have no use for no ugly woman. And that is fat or slim! When you wake up in the morning and you head ain't settle yet, you ain't want to turn and see a face that could stop you heart from beat."

"So you think I pretty or you making talks?"

"Baby, if I make talks to you, you'd ask me to marry you right now. My talks is like a sweet rum punch. It nice you when it going down, but when you done you feel regret, 'cause it will drunk you and make you give away you life."

"So I pretty then?"

"Like the moon right there."

She leaned forward and craned her head and saw it. It was bright and almost full, and as she felt it pulling at romantic feelings in her liquid depths, the driver asked her faintly, "I could touch you leg?"

56

"I don't think so," she said, then fired: "Touch my leg for what?"

Respectfully, he answered, "So I could give a good accounting to my son."

The moon illuminated certain passions. She was grateful for the ride, and flattered that he'd choose her for his son. Plus the cab felt oddly safe, safe in the way of a studio, a place in which to probe around. Try new things. Test limits. Rehearse.

"But don't go too far," she said, and dropped her forearm in the crevice where her pelvis met her thigh. The driver's touch was quick and light, more a test of ripeness than a fondle or caress. She took his hand and held it and they rode in swollen silence for a while.

When they reached the intersection with the coastal road he came around to help her from the cab.

"You're a beautiful girl," he told her. "My son deserves a girl like you. Some men ain't like a girl with lip. But I like a little lip. Is the ones who ain't like to talk I can't take. See ... if they ain't like to talk, they like to brood. I can't take a woman who just stare at you over breakfast when she vex. When they look at you that brooding way, you lose the taste for food. When a woman gimme lip I take it, smile, then eat my blasted food. But when they stare at me like that, oh God." He felt he'd said too much and tapped her on the chin. "But look. I running. God bless you. I glad you make me change my mind."

"A man never tell me I beautiful, you know, so I don't know what to say."

Across the street she saw the orange light of bottle torches glowing in the stalls where old *negritas* dressed in skirts and turbans sold small fritters made from black-eyed peas and served with pepper sauce, along with cuts of fried shark. She could also see the silhouettes of dogs and milling people, and smell the garlic marinade in which the cuts of shark were left to soak all day before the old *negritas* dipped them in the cornmeal batter, turning them to make the grainy mixture cream the meat, which they'd slide into the iron pots that had been used by their grandmothers, and the batter-covered meat would settle in the oily depths where all the salty flavour lurked and gain a brittle shell.

Beneath the smell of fish there was the wheaty fragrance of the heavy bread the fat *negritas* baked in ovens built from lime and brick right there beside the road, round loaves that came out bronzed and dusty with the smoky taste of coals.

Estrella was warmed by all of this – the smell of food, her conversation and the sound of happy voices crackling like a splash of water dripping in hot oil.

Her head began to sink towards her shoulder when the driver stepped up on the running board and sat alone inside the cab.

"If you ever pass again, come by the distillery gate and ask for me," he said. "Xavier Joseph. Everybody know me down there. Just call my name."

She wanted to say something romantic, but all the words she thought about just felt so damn untrue.

"If you ever get a message that a girl name Cinderella by the gate," she said, believing that the meaning would be lost on him, "you'll bound to know is me."

They looked at each other the way people do when time begins to curl and stretch as if it were a lazy cat.

"Come," he said, and slapped the door. "Lemme take you further down."

They quickly left the stalls behind, and moved along a flat, unpopulated coast. The road held closely to the water, which she heard above the engine, breaking on the reef. It was a long, straight beach with hardly any curves, and the water was so clear that in the daytime you could see the shadows of the fish against the ocean's rippled floor. The sand was so white that on the coolest days you had to squint to see it, and so dry that people said it had been blown there by a desert wind.

She wanted him to try to hold her hand again, and was a little disappointed that he didn't reach.

Suppose he was just holding my hand to make me feel good? she thought. Suppose he ain't even have no son. But nothing ain't wrong with that. Nothing ain't wrong if a person tell a little lie to make another person feel okay. I do it all the time. Maybe he was asking for himself. Sometimes them old man have some crafty ways. But it felt good all the same. He touch me nice. I was feeling little wetty when he touch my leg in truth. But you know what? I ain't want to tie up my head with no stupidness. I have important things to do.

But she was young and disappointed and couldn't help herself.

"Why you being so nice to me?"

"You know if they catch me with my headlights on they lock me up?"

"So why you ain't turn back?"

"Is blackout time now, you know. If they catch me now is grief."

"So why you going so far out o' you way to do something for me? You ain't know me. And I ain't know you. And I ain't make no kind o' promise to you."

"Sometimes in life you shouldn't ask so much," he said. "Sometimes you should just take the ride."

"I think you say you like woman with lip?"

In his mind he said, *But I like them more with hip.*

Aloud, he said: "How old are you, Miss Cinderella? In truth how old are you?"

"Old enough," she softly taunted.

"Girl, talk to me in a serious fashion. How old are you?"

"Pick a number."

"Okay, let's call it sixteen. When you turn into a big woman and have children and all that, you going realise something. When you is a pretty woman, you could get a man to do all kind o' things. You could get a man to work all his money and come and give you like you name is bank."

"You so full o' talks," she said. With an elbow on the door she'd begun to stroke her hair.

"Well, I is a old man. What you expect?"

"They say is better to be a old man darling than a young boy slave," she offered, playing at being adult.

"Well, is who full o' talks now? Me or you?"

"That ain't talks, man. That is truth."

"You know what is true?" he tested, as the tyres crushed a mob of crabs caught crawling in the road. "Maybe I shouldn't tell you anything 'bout my son. Maybe I should keep you for myself."

"But how you could keep what you ain't have?"

She resettled herself in her seat.

"So what it take?"

He reached for her. She eased away, but let him hold her hand.

"I ain't know," she answered as she squeezed his palm. "Nobody ain't catch me yet."

"So what it would take?"

His foot had left the pedal and the truck began to slow.

"I ain't know," she said, and shook him loose. "Drive up. Drive up, fast."

"Tell me," he said sincerely, "and I promise to do it for you."

When she saw now that she'd broken him, her skin began to tingle with the warm electric current of a thrill, and she told him in a bossy way, "Well, take me into town."

"I can't do that," he mumbled with regret. "I ain't have the petrol in the tank."

"But you care for me," she said, the bossiness receding from her voice.

"I ain't know you long. But in this short, short time, I do."

"Don't make it spoil then." There was a part of her that wasn't sure if what he'd said about his tank was true. "Here's what you do. Stop the truck right here and touch me 'pon my leg again and call me beautiful. Don't do one then do the next. Don't touch then talk. Do the two o' them together. And when you finish, put me out and wish me luck. I'll do the same to you." She kissed her palm and pressed it to his cheek. "You make me feel real nice, yes. And I ain't want that niceness to spoil. 'Cause it always spoil. It always spoil. Thank you very much."

VIII.

The road was dark and silent, and she focused on the slapping of her feet against the asphalt as she walked. In the distance, she could hear the engine fading and the short compression coming just before the elongation of the gears, a pattern like a snore. She hummed to rinse the loss before it stained.

There was grass along the verge, and as her eyes adjusted to the moonlight, she could see a narrow path.

Shit ... I ain't know what in them grass, she thought, standing in the road. Them grass could have all kind o' *macka* to jam me in my foot. And it have some worse than snakebite, I hear. Those, when they jam you, make you foot swell so much you feel like you walking with a ball and chain. The road hard, and my foot feel soft, but I ain't able for no swell foot tonight – especially how my driver gone.

Her conversation with Joseph had left her feeling sentimental, and now, for the first time in her life, she felt uneasy in the dark. Like a novice sailor in a boat caught up in big waves, she couldn't find a way to put herself along an even keel. And her skin began to prickle as she grudgingly admitted that she, Estrella Thompson, a castaway, was something precious that someone could lose. Her life was not her own. It belonged to all who showed her love. Like the woman in the red bandanna and Vashti, the handsome man with the rash along his face. Like Joseph. Even Asif!

It would matter if they woke up in the morning and heard that something awful had occurred ... that she'd been robbed or killed or raped. If something awful happened it would count. She began to feel now that she should have talked to Joseph more to find out

what it would have cost to take her into town. If it had come to it
... if he'd said he'd do it but her body was the price, she would
have paid it, she was thinking, would have found a way to make
it work. Maybe she would have asked him to repeat that she was
pretty while he touched her leg as if it were a length of rich,
imported cloth. Maybe she would have touched herself and
thought of someone else while he was sliding in on top of her ...
just so she wouldn't have to be alone ... just so that she wouldn't
be the one in charge of making sure that nothing awful happened,
of making sure that sadness didn't flood these people's lives.

One mile. Two miles. Three miles. Four. She walked without
seeing a soul. Sometimes she saw dim flickers and heard voices,
and knew she was passing by a hut set back into the bush.
Sometimes a shadow in a larger clump beside the verge would
break away and she'd recognise the blotchy outline of a moving
thing. When she thought it was human she'd say goodnight.
If she thought it was a ghost she'd cross herself and pray.

Eventually, the beach gave way to cattle country and the road
began to swerve. As it swerved, it drifted and began to change its
course, and Estrella found herself being pressed on either side by
humps of aromatic pasture tipped with chimneyed houses and
rectangled by fences of stone.

I know for sure where I going now, she thought, on seeing the
houses, which were silhouetted on the slightly lighter sky. When
I make it, that's the kind o' house I going buy. Far away on top of
a hill where nobody ain't have to know my business, and I could
see if anybody coming to interfere with me and send my dog to
bite them. You getting to town soon. Not soon like *soon*. But
soon. You moving. You not staying behind. When you see things
like a fence it mean you close to people who know that things
can't just be wild like that, that you have to set them so they have
a proper look like lines you see in books. And you only find them
kind o' people in town.

As Estrella walked, a sour taste began to creep into her throat and she sat on a stone. She'd eaten some mangoes as she'd waited on the bridge; now the juice had fermented, and the acid burned her stomach walls.

I tell you ... sand ain't easy when it hot, she thought, rubbing her aching feet. But if you put you mind against it you could bear it. Them paved roads that it have here ain't easy – hot or cold. This town thing going take some getting used to. To live in town ... even if you only manage to get a simple job ... even if you don't get to reach you ambition ... even if all you going get to do is walk around and sell peanut or newspaper, you going have to get a pair o' shoes.

As she'd done when she'd been travelling on the bus, she took her bearings by projecting out to sea, and gathered that she was a little under thirteen miles from town.

Walking again, her nostrils caught a trace of smoke. It was too dark to see the columns in the sky. And in truth it could have come from someone cooking late at night or burning coal. But there were disturbances in Black Well, she remembered. And Black Well was directly on the way.

As she wondered if there was another route, she heard the clop and scrape of iron shoes behind her. Turning now, she saw the shadow of a rider on a horse.

"Begging a ride," she called out from thirty yards away. "Please, if you could help me. I'm begging you a ride."

The rider waited till he'd drawn his horse beside her.

"Who is that?" he asked in Spanish. "How do I know you're not a thief?"

She was standing by a tree that overgrew a fence, and though the rider was ten feet from her she couldn't see his face. But from his voice, which had a rasp, as if his vocal cords were made of rope, and from the fact that he was speaking Spanish – which she understood but couldn't repeat – Estrella knew he was *criollo* from the South Atlantic coast, a descendant of the early Spanish settlers who'd accepted British rule.

"I ain't no thief," she said in *Sancoche*, a slave-born bastard child of Spanish. "If I was a thief I wouldn't call you from afar. I would bide my time and wait until you passing easy, like everything is fine, and then I'd knock you off you horse."

She imagined that he had a tapered face and skin the colour of the waterpots his people made from clay – and she was right. His hair was dark, and he wore it in a *cola* – a lengthy ponytail – partly hidden by his hat, a black fedora.

"I know the horse tired," she persisted, "but my feet is tired more, and they ain't stony like you horse's foot that wearing iron shoes."

The horse stomped. The movement scared her and she jumped away.

"How old are you?" the horseman asked in Spanish, leaning over.

"Old enough."

"Old enough for what? It's very late," he told her in a curt, officious way. "I'm sure you know there's a curfew. Where's your mother? A girl your age should be at home."

"I ain't no child," she said. "And I ain't live with my mother for a long, long time."

He got off his horse and tied it to a limb of the overhanging tree and leaned against the long stone fence.

He was an experienced seducer who understood that women fell in love through words, and whenever he met a prospect, he'd take the time to find out what she liked to talk about. In his district he was famous for remarking, "If you listen, you will learn."

"Nice night," he said matter-of-factly. "Look at that beautiful moon."

"I been watching at it all night."

"What do you think of when you see a moon like this?"

"That night is darker than day."

"You don't like to talk about the moon?"

"It have other things I like to talk 'bout more."

"Like what?" he asked indulgently.

"Nothing I can bring my mind to think 'bout right now. Right now, all I can think 'bout is getting into town while the moon is in the sky. Because when sun come is morning."

"Did the horse frighten you?"

"I frighten, yes. I think I see 'bout four ghosts on this road tonight. My nerves ain't able for no excitement."

Oh, he told himself, she's afraid.

"I am very sorry," he told her. "He is a strange horse, you know. A faithful one too. Whenever he gets a feeling that I might be in danger, he tries to warn me that I should escape."

"Horse have so much sense?" she said, her intellect aroused.

He eased up from the fence and paced the verge with his long, slim legs. He was short, but high-waisted, and wore a denim workshirt and tan trousers, which were tucked into his knee-length riding boots.

"This is not an ordinary horse," he told her, improvising on a story he'd often told before. "First of all, he is a police horse. He was trained by the police. All my family is police, you know. And this horse was a good police horse. Strong horse. Faithful horse. But he got a damage to his foot."

He heard Estrella laugh with recognition as he shifted from Spanish to *Sancoche*.

"You smell smoke?" he asked, sniffing loudly.

"A little bit," she said.

"Trouble," he said mysteriously.

"What kind o' trouble?"

"Black Well hot tonight. That is a place I can't understand. They always having some excitement." He shook his head. "You see that same Black Well where the smoke coming from? Right down in there. That's where it happened. This horse took a policeman down in there when they had a disturbance and one o' those wild people – 'cause they *wild*, you know – just all of a sudden jump up and swing a machete. The edge was going to take his head. But at the last moment the horse rear up and took the chop on his front leg. *Bam!* And you know that after all those years o' service the police was going to shoot him? But I was there at the time. And I jump up and say, 'No! You shouldn't do that. This is a good horse and a faithful horse, a horse you can always trust.' And I told them I would keep it and care it. And look at the horse now." As if apologising, he paused and said, "Well, if it was day you could really see what I talking 'bout. A damn fine horse as you'd ever see."

The passion. The engagement. The details. The drama. The way he told the story made her think of Joseph. Now she felt as if she knew the rider better than she did, and because of this suspended disbelief.

"When you go through a lot and people help you, you have to be grateful," she said in deep reflection. "Even a horse could know that. But it have some people in this world, you know, sir, who never learn that lesson in their life."

"You are one of those?"

"No sir. Not at all."

"What kind o' person you is?"

"Oh. It hard to say. I never have to answer any question like that in my life before." Then after she'd thought about her day she said, "Unlucky."

"Well, you luck might change tonight."

"Gimme a ride and maybe I'll believe."

He made a noncommittal exclamation.

"Well, it was nice to meet you," he said, in Spanish again. "All the best and good luck."

He began to untie the horse.

"Which part you going?" she asked in mild panic.

"Town," he said, as if from deep inside a thought. "Seville."

"Then I could get a ride?" She held him by the arm. "I thought you was stopping because you was going to give me a ride."

"He's an old horse," the man said with false compassion. "And his leg is still not very good. And I'm not sure if he likes you." He paused as if to think. "No ... I don't think he can take the weight."

Nervous, she began to stroke the horse along the neck to show that she was liked.

"See there. He ain't mind me at all."

"But the weight ... the weight ... the weight."

"I don't weigh plenty," she said. "Come. Weigh me."

He reached for her and held her close and ran his hand along the length of her, pretending that he couldn't find a grip. She was firm and tight with even curves, and as he lifted her, he paused and dipped her twice so that her little breasts would brush against his nose.

But although she was smooth and had a subtle give, the girl was densely muscled, and the man began to struggle with her weight. While wobbling, he softly slapped her flank, which signalled her to wrap her legs around him, giving both of them the pleasure of a quick embrace.

"Okay," he murmured when he'd set her down. "Okay. You can come."

With this, he lifted her as one would lift a bride, and placed her on the horse.

Accustomed to a kind of easy gruffness all her life, and feeling tender in the dark, she assented when he used his hand to draw her back into the armchair comfort of his chest.

The horse wasn't covered with a saddle, and she found it hard to keep her balance on the padding made of sugar sacks.

"You okay?" he asked her when the horse began to move. "You 'fraid?"

"I feel high," she said, too scared to turn her head in case the movement made her fall.

"You want me to hold you?"

"I feeling okay for a while."

"When he start to trot it going be kind o' rough. And the way you was talking I think you want to reach town really quick."

"When you talk about trot and all that, it have me a little nervous," she confessed. "He could see where he going? How he know where he going in the dark? Next thing something frighten him and he throw we off."

He slipped an arm around her waist and used one hand to hold the rope.

"This horse is a good horse," he said. "As long as he don't think you want to fight me or nothing, he will do the best for you."

When he felt as if she'd settled on the brawny colt, he asked, "So what you going to town to do?"

She answered brightly, "Improve myself and find a work."

"What kind o' work you can do?"

"I could do any kind o' work," she said. "I ain't 'fraid hard work, you know. As long as people ain't try to bamboozle me and get me in any kind o' tug-o'-war, I could do anything."

"Whoa! Whoa! Whoa!"

He startled her.

"What happen?"

"Take your time. Slow down. Everybody ain't from the countryside. I know *Sancoche*, but when you give it that backward twang you throw me."

"Not because you gimme a ride you could insult me, you know, sir. I begging you a ride and I grateful for it, but I could walk my walk and reach where I going. I ain't take insult."

But when all this had left her mouth, she thought, You need to learn to hold you tongue. Suppose the man get vex and put you off, what you going do? The road hard. The way long. *Bangarang* down in Black Well. Tell the man you sorry. As old-time people say, when you hand in a lion mouth, take you time and pull it out.

"Mister ..." she began, before he interrupted with, "I'm sorry."

He said it in a way designed to touch her heart ... mannish in his voice but childish in his tone.

Before she could speak again, he added: "I didn't mean to insult you."

"Well, it was an ungrateful thing to say," she said. "And I'm not ungrateful. Believe me. I just tired."

"I'm tired too," he replied, and placed his chin beside her neck. "We're two tired people. We're both sorry that we're tired. We have so much in common that we'd make such good friends. Let's do that. That's what I want to do. I just want to ride with you and be your friend, and talk to you and get to know you. I want to know the way you think."

She smiled. The movement of the horse beneath her was a mounting pleasure; but more importantly, the man had made her feel that he'd perceived her as a person with a mind.

"What you want to know?"

She squeezed a shoulder to her ear.

"I want to know about ... you," he half-stuttered. "About how you feel in general ... about life."

In English, the language of all things important and bright, she said, "I think to be boring is one of the most awful things that could happen in life." In truth, she meant "bored".

"Are you an exciting person?" he asked in English more fluent than hers.

"I think so. But I just haven't got the chance to do a lot of things I really want to do."

"Like what?" he asked warmly.

"Like to go to Europe."

Her mind began to drift. And while she saw herself arriving in a car at La Sala and working in a store, and eating only beef and chicken at her meals and feeding fish and lobsters to her dog, the rider gripped the stallion tightly with his knees and ground against her flanks.

Getting no resistance, he slid a hand along her leg, which felt damp and firm and outward-curved with strength beneath her long blue skirt. With his thumb, he traced it where it had a solid crease along the side, where down below, he knew, there lurked the heavy bone.

"How much is for a pair o' shoes in town?" she asked, distracted, returning to *Sancoche*.

He quickly moved his hands. She'd begun to shift her weight as if she'd just awoken from a dream.

"Are you comfy?" he asked. "You seem unsettled."

"I don't know," she told him. "Maybe is because I know that Black Well coming up."

"Oh. I thought you'd leaned against my pistol."

"Oh. You have a gun?"

"Not that we'll need to use it. I could walk through Black Well any time."

He leaned away from her and fussed around his waist and made a mental count, then uttered, "There."

"That feels better," she told him when he eased her back to lean on him again.

"Now what kind o' shoes you would like?"

She paused to think. Accustomed to the horse by now, she turned her head to speak.

"The kind you wear to work in a office or a shop."

"I ain't mean to be rude," he said, "but you have money to buy shoes?"

He tapped her with his boots against her heel.

"I might," she answered in a way she thought of as *mysteriously*. In fact it was *vague, as if she had no clue at all*.

"You ain't really know town, do you?" he asked in a sympathetic voice.

"What you trying to say? Of course."

He didn't challenge her, but proceeded in a tone that said that any difference of opinion when it came to town had little consequence because his perspective was right.

"I ain't mean to disappoint you, but them fuckers – excuse my language – ain't like to give *negritas* certain jobs, you know ... in banks and office and shops. But you know this already of course."

"I ain't care what they like to do," she said. "I just want to know what shoes you have to have to work there."

"Well, being that I used to own a store," he said, in English now, "I know a thing or two. Everybody else in my family are police, as I told you. That is one of the ways how I was able to get this .38. Be that as it may, I am the only one who had the head for business. But that too is for another day. Back to your question about shoes. You can't just wear any shoes when you work in a place of business, you know. You have to wear the finest shoes. And the finest shoes in the world are English shoes. You can't go for the kind of job you're talking about in Spanish shoes or American shoes." He slapped his thigh for emphasis. "No way. Wear one of those and the boss will take one look at you and say you don't know what you're doing."

"For true?"

"Absolutely. Now why would I lie to you?"

"No. I'm not saying you is a liar, sir. Is just a phrase."

"I know it's just a phrase, sweetheart. But so is 'Why would I lie to you?'"

"Oh."

"I know about English shoes, you know. I know so much I could write a book. I know the English very well. I met a lot of them when I lived in Europe."

"Really!"

She was so excited that she tried to turn around to face him. She lost her balance and he held her waist, then found and squeezed her hand.

With his fingers playing on her palm, he said: "I used to live there for a very long time."

He said this in the kind of breathy tone in which a singer introduces certain kinds of sentimental songs, and she reacted with the gush of folks who purchase tickets for those certain kinds of shows.

"Where?" she asked him. "Which part? Tell me."

"Paris," he said. "Then after I lived in Paris, I moved ..."

"To where?"

"Oh, after Paris ... let me see ... I lived in so many different places. Oh ... after Paris I moved to France."

"And what about the war?" she asked. It struck her that she hadn't read the news. "You see the war?"

"*See* the war?" he chortled. "*See* the war? My love, I *fought* the war!"

"Oh Jesus Christ."

"That's why you need to listen when I talk. That's why when I tell you about shoes you should never doubt me. You need English shoes, my friend, and those shoes are expensive. How much money do you have on you right now? How much could you put down on a counter for a pair of top-class English shoes?"

"Five pounds," she said with force.

The man exploded in deep-throated laughter.

"That can't buy it?" she asked with doubt, revealing that she didn't know that she was right.

More excited now, he laughed again.

"Okay, then ... fourteen pounds. I could walk into one o' them stores and fling down fourteen pounds on that counter and say, 'Gimme you best pair o' goddamn English shoes. I have fourteen pounds on me right now.'"

He stopped the horse and put both arms around the girl.

"Good shoes like that cost forty pounds," he said. "With fourteen pounds you couldn't even buy a single foot."

Estrella Thompson raised her head to calm herself, then dropped her chin and cried.

"But it's not the end of the world," he added in a fatherly way. "Oh, hush."

"It ain't you feeling pain. So you can say what you want."

"I know pain," he improvised. "I know a kind of pain I hope you'll never understand. Look ..."

He allowed his voice to fade.

"What happen to you?" she asked him, working to control her breath.

"I don't want to talk."

"What happen?"

"I ... just don't want ..."

"Tell me?"

Her voice was creamy like a soft eruption.

"I want to. But I can't."

"Yes, you can. You have to try."

"I know, but ..."

She told him sternly: "Do you know how many times I want someone to hear me and it ain't nobody there?" She held his arms and used her weight to rock them. "I thought you said you wanted me and you to be good friends?"

He sighed. He hummed. He moaned. Then said, "When they shoot me in the war, you don't think it hurt? It hurt so bad. It hurt so bad. It hurt so goddamn bad. As I talk about it now, I

74

feel the pain as if it was happening again." She felt him shiver. "I thought I was going to die. Death is not a easy thing. When it stare you in the face, you ain't want to see it close again. And that's how it feel when you talk about it."

"I know it hard to talk about, but ... what happened?"

"Three Japanese ambush me in Berlin. But I got them though. They thought I was dead. But I saw them running in the dark. And as I lie down there, thinking that was it, I shoot them down like birds."

"In the dark?"

"In the dark. Dark night just like this. Well, not so dark, but noisy. Fighting is a cantankerous thing."

With this, he got off the horse and walked away.

"Where you going?" she cried. "I ain't want this horse to run away with me ... and ... and how you doing down there?"

She couldn't see him in the dark, and she imagined rightly that his arms were raised towards the gods.

"I am a damn disgrace!" he screamed towards the sky. "I am nothing but a big disgrace!"

"What you mean? No. That ain't true."

"Of course I am. I should be taking care o' you to *rass* and instead o' doing that I'm crying like a baby. Oh lord. This thing called war is hell."

She stumbled off the horse and groped towards his voice.

"You can't leave the horse alone," he called out, as he took a path towards a spot he often used.

Estrella led the horse towards the rider's heavy breathing till she felt his hand against hers in the dark.

She left him with the horse and went to stand some yards away, allowing him the privacy to cry. Her whole being felt exposed and tender, and her fourteen-year-old heart was full of sympathy and awe for this traveller, this soldier, this stranger who'd come to her rescue, this gentleman who'd lifted her and placed her on his brave and faithful horse and tried to get to know her as he took her to the place where she'd get a chance to fix her damn unlucky life.

"What is your name?" she heard him asking from behind.

"Estrella," she said. "Estrella Thompson is my name. And what is yours?"

"Simón," he said. "Simón ... Simón ... Bolívar."

She said in English, "That's a wonderful, beautiful name."

"And you, my love, are a beautiful, beautiful girl."

"How do you know? You never seen me."

"Because ... beautiful people have beautiful ... they're just beautiful all over. Come here. I want to use my hands to know your beautiful, lovely face."

"Do you find me interesting?" she asked.

He sat on a stone at the foot of a tree.

"Of course," he said. "Of course."

He placed a cheek against her stomach, touched and stroked her face, then slid his hands across her body from her shoulders to her thighs. She removed his hat and rubbed his head as if he were her nameless wooden dolly come to life.

"I'm so sorry about what happened in the war," she said, delighting in the texture of his silken hair.

The rider stood and shrugged and slouched around the tree, knowing she would follow. She slipped her arms around his neck and felt his body stiffen in her tight embrace. There was a near maternal softness to his middle, an endearing strangeness in a slender man.

She pressed her diamond face against his chest. He smelled of rum and cedar shavings and carbolic soap, but none of them intensely. When she squeezed herself between his arms she felt secure, as if her tender feelings grew an instant shell.

The rider was a man of patience, and he held her without moving. When he was certain that her feelings wouldn't change,

76

he sent his strong hands sliding down her sides and up again as potters do with clay.

"Why you touching me like you want something?" she asked him in her awkward country way.

They'd been kissing slowly for several minutes, and he'd placed her hand against his pants while she stroked the thing she found there till it felt as solid as an ear of corn.

"If you offered me something I would take it," he said as they stroked each other. "But I would never ask."

"Beg me the right way and maybe I give you."

His hands were masters exercising their control. One was sweeping down along her side, around her back, swooping with her spine. The other one had reached beneath her skirt and was touching her so lightly that it felt as if he meant to finely sand the rims of muscle slanting from the cleavage of her bottom to her thighs.

"You are so finely made," he whispered. "So finely fashioned. Jesus was a carpenter. He made you out of wood."

"But look how you mouth full o' sweet talks," she said. "And still you won't come out and tell me what you want."

"You know what I want," he told her.

"Well, touch it then. If you dumb, you dumb. Come on, dummy. Touch it. Show Mama what you want."

He paused, overwhelmed. He was accustomed to women who were coy.

"You 'fraid?" she softly taunted. "Like how you big horse scare me, my little catty make you scared? Big man like you who fight war and thing? Who kill man and thing? A little catty ain't supposed to frighten you."

"Put my hand on it."

As she led his hand into the clenching hump of fur between her legs, he used the other one to pull her buttons, starting from her neck.

When the blouse had been undone, he ran his hands along the curving, rising length of her sea-strengthened smoothness. Amazed by its perfection, he laughed.

"What sweet you?" she asked.

"I just don't know what else to do."

He unhooked her frayed brassiere.

She told him: "Take care. Mind the pins."

He obeyed, and she slipped out of her skirt and hung it with her blouse and undergarments on a limb above her head.

"But we have to make haste," she told him, then turned around and gripped the tree and hoisted up a leg.

"No, no, darling. Take your time and face me."

When she'd placed her back against the tree, he knelt before her with his trousers tucked into his long black boots, held her by the hips, and swept his tongue across the rosy droplet barely sagging from her pubic hairs, and she sputtered like he'd thrown her overboard while she was sleeping.

"Did I frighten you?"

His head was clamped between her knees.

If Simón take his hands from me right now, Estrella thought, I going fall down in a pile. I never feel nothing like this before. It feel like he pull out all my bones. Or like my body was a shaking tooth and he just play with it till it nearly turn to pain.

If you frighten me? Yes, you frighten me, yes. Because any man who could do this to me could wreck my blasted life. Could have me thinking 'bout this and nothing else. Make me stay home instead o' going to work in the morning. And I ain't want nobody rule me like that. I ain't want nobody rule me with nothing at all. And how the *rass* I come to this? How it go from talking to something like this? This ain't what I out for – taking man in bush.

"I have to put on my clothes," she said, reaching for the limb. The faucet of emotion was turned off. "You okay?"

"Is this some kind o' joke?"

He staggered to his feet in disbelief.

She couldn't find the pin for her brassiere and she grumbled as she looked, talking to herself, cursing just beneath her breath as if he weren't there. She gave up trying to find the pin in the dark and slipped on her skirt before she stepped inside her bloomers – a habit that had started when Old Tuck had nearly caught her with a boy.

Dressed, she stuffed the bra in the pocket with her money and her knife.

"How long till we reach town?"

"Walking," he answered, "a very, very, very long time."

"Don't get sulky and contrary now," she said across her shoulder as she walked towards the horse. "Come visit me tomorrow at my place in town."

Estrella wasn't being dishonest. She was playing at being adult – reaching forward into what she wished to be her coming life, a life in which she'd have the means to live alone and have the privacy to entertain whenever she might please.

"Don't play me for a fool," the rider said.

With long strides he overtook her. His voice was soft but stiff in tone; his shoulders taut and hunched.

"I'm not trying to bamboozle, you," she reassured him. "But time going fast."

"We can do it very quickly," he insisted. "Why start and stop like this? Why tomorrow? We're here right now."

This is what I can't take, she thought. Now everything gone and spoil. I have to work out where I going sleep and all he want to do is fuck. If he could wait awhile I might give him a little thing. But I have to see where I laying my head tonight. It have a few place down by the waterfront that them sailors use. I wonder how much for those? It can't be too much. And I only need it for the night. But anything you spend to get a room, she told herself, is taking money from you shoes. Now what going happen with that?

"Simón," she asked, "how much for the English ones again?"

"I really don't care anymore. I hope you get to where you're going safely. I'm gone."

"Listen, Simón," Estrella bluffed. "Since you ride me on that horse and my feet get to relax, I could march with Mr Hitler army from Tokyo to Japan and ain't care. You hear me? So don't talk to me 'bout how you going ride away and leave me. Everything have its time. And every time have its thing. And this is not the time for no more thing. You understand?"

"I have a thing," he said, and took her by the arm. "Does it have a time as well?"

"I ain't know," she answered as she tried to pull away. She was separated from her basket. If she didn't have it then she couldn't run away.

"Simón," she reasoned, feeling the heavy body of the horse against her back, "you was going somewhere. Wherever you was going you have to get there. You ain't have no time for this. I tell you tomorrow. Then let it be tomorrow, nuh. Why so much of a haste?"

"If we're going to fuck, let's fuck," he muttered. "Are we going to fuck?"

"I ain't like that kind o' language, Simón. I really ain't like it at all. A nice man like you shouldn't say those things, Simón. They ain't suit a gentleman like you."

His breath was hot against her face. The horse was firm against her back. A presence like a wall. She was about to bite the rider, then remembered that he'd talked about a gun.

If you take the knife and stab him you could get away, she thought. But what going happen after that? All his family is police. They going lock you up. You is a outcast. Ain't nobody coming to talk for you. And even so, what you grandmother and

Big Tuck could do? I born unlucky. I born fucking unlucky to *rass*. Lemme rub my thighs and see. I still a little wetty. I could turn my mind to something else.

"Come," she said abruptly. "Since you have to fuck me, let's fuck. But don't take too damn long."

She reached under her skirt and tugged away her bloomers and grumbled as he kissed her on the neck.

"But can you just pretend?"

"Simón, pretend that what?"

"That ... that you like this. That you like me."

"But after this I won't like you no more. Because everything have to be how you want it. You don't give me any consideration. I really have to get to town. I tell you we can do this tomorrow. But *your* tomorrow have to come and mash up my today. I wish I could say I ain't like you, Simón. If it was so, this wouldn't be so bad."

"Look ... I'm sorry."

"Don't confuse me. Just be fast."

She stomped across the grass towards the tree.

"Maybe we should lie down in the grass," he told her sweetly. "I want to lie on you and touch you. I don't want to be like any beast."

"Look, I wash my hair today and all sort o' things on that ground, and I don't have no more change o' clothes. I ain't doing this because I want to do this, Simón. Is because this is how it have to be. Push it in. Do it now so we can go."

"Don't be savage."

She was resisting his control and he was worried that she was about to change her mind again – slam it like a door. And in the anonymity of the darkness, in the isolated wildness of the bush, with the feel and taste of her as distinct as a sharp voice egging him on, he accepted that he didn't have the nerve to pry her open, even though he felt a coiled emotion that he thought might be the urge. The discordant echo of his clashing feelings rang and hummed along his bones, feeding back distortion to his moral core, amplifying everything till all he could hear inside his head was one gigantic, primal roar of shame.

"Don't insult me, Simón, or I going stop right now."

"Can't you just be nice?"

"To who?"

"Stop talking. You're making this worse."

As she leaned against the tree, she thought, Look at what I come to. I really born unlucky. Look. I have the proof.

She didn't fight him when he hooked one of her thighs beneath the knee, and the truth is that he didn't hold her in a forceful way.

They proceeded with the strained cooperation of a pair of office clerks. She did what she could but nothing more, moving every now and then; and when he tried to kiss her, she would turn so that his lips would skid across her cheeks. When he dipped and tried to put her knee across his shoulder, she didn't let her body help him with the weight, and she grumbled when he sucked his teeth and clamped her thigh against his ribs. Her resistance was unnerving, and he found himself existing in a dim suspended state of neither pleasure nor disgust, suffering through a kind of stultifying rote, wishing he could come ... in and out ... out and in ... like sorting bags of mail.

Twenty minutes later, when he still wasn't done, she reached into her pocket for her knife and pressed the point behind his ear.

"Simón, is either I put down my leg or you finish right now."

"One more. Don't kill me. Two more. Please wait."

"Stop it, Simón. Stop it. You ain't feeling how I dry?"

The danger of the knife against him brought the rider's feelings to an edge, so when she shouted that she'd slit his throat, he felt the vertigo of falling and the urge to give her anything she wanted in the world.

"You want the shoes, my love?"

"Just finish."

"Reach around the back into my wallet. It have ten or twenty pounds."

It was a little after midnight when they rode into Seville, which was dark and unreflective like a glass of port. Under blackout orders, all lights were off, all curtains drawn, and the smoke that blew from Black Well dimmed the glitter of the moon.

The balance of the journey had been passed in silence. Their lips were sealed by shame. When they'd got on the horse again, he'd let her sit behind him so he wouldn't have to face the fact that she was there.

Estrella wasn't sure if she'd been raped. She'd been overpowered, she knew, but not with anything she knew as force; after all, she'd been the one to pull the knife.

Maybe I just worthless in truth, she told herself. I like to say I unlucky. But maybe I just worthless in truth. So you have a knife and he ain't beat you. He ain't put no gun to you. He ain't put you on no ground. And then he give you money and you take it. That ain't sound like rape when you put it like that. That sound like *whore* to me.

Maybe I ain't really know myself in truth. Maybe them people at the cove know me better than I really know myself. Maybe them old people see things in me I ain't really see. Them dirty parts. Them nasty parts. Them worthless parts.

If I never take the money, I wonder if I'd feel a different way? I ain't know. I ain't know. But I can't give it back. It ain't make no sense. If I give it back I going feel like nothing never come from it. Like I ain't get nothing for my pain. 'Cause what I feeling right now is pain. Which one carry more shame? A damn prostitute or a careless girl that get rape? I ain't really know ...

She spent the balance of the journey in deep deliberation. Either way, the people of the cove would say she'd got all that she deserved, and her name would be a watermark for years to come. *Continue on your ways and end up like Estrella. Go on. Continue. You will see.*

When they'd come across the iron bridge that led into the town, Estrella felt a gradual lightening of her mood, and she consoled herself by saying that everything between the cove and town had been sacrificial acts, and she paid homage to all the powers that she knew ... God, the *orishas*, the abstract unseen ... and told herself that she was not alone, that Vashti and Joseph and the woman with the red bandanna would be sad if they knew what had happened ... that she was beautiful and precious ... that she'd be missed if she were taken from this world.

"I'm sorry," said the rider when he helped her off the horse before the statue of Horatio Nelson. Behind her was the lapping harbour. Across the street, behind him, were rows of old buildings on Nelson Square.

"I have it in my heart to forgive you," she said, "but I ain't going lie – it going be harder to forgive myself."

"I don't know what to do."

"I ain't ask you for nothing," she said blankly, scooping sand over the fragile memories, hiding them like turtle eggs. "I have twenty extra pounds. I ask for a ride and you gimme a ride. At the time, I just ain't know the price."

"I hope you get your shoes," he said. "I hope they're strong. I hope they fit you good."

"And I hope you get what you deserve. I get my share tonight."

He touched her hand, and for reasons that she didn't fully comprehend, she drew him close and kissed him quickly, hoping that he'd do something to make her think that what she thought of him was wrong – unsure of what she'd take as proof.

She squinted hard to watch him mount the horse, but she didn't watch him ride away.

It began to drizzle, and she made her way across the street into the square. In the dark, she picked her way along a cobbled path that sprayed out from the fountain, taking shelter on a bench beneath a tree.

When the rain began to really pour, she dashed into the portal of a colonnaded building on the square.

Nelson Square, the oldest part of the town, was a collection of fine buildings, some in marble, some in coral stone, constructed in the 1600s – in San Carlos, a period of excess at the height of Spanish rule. Many of them had columns, stained glass and Moorish courtyards, evoking larger, grander squares in Old Havana.

One side of the square was open to the sea; two sides were closed and the third was dominated by a large brick building with a grand archway that opened on the Queens, the boulevard that rose along the row of former mansions to the governor's gate, the address of Salan's and La Sala de Amor – the emporium and restaurant of her dreams.

In her blue skirt and green-striped blouse damp with man smell, sweat and rain, Estrella Thompson found a spot beside the high stone steps of the court. Before she fell asleep she took her brassiere from her pocket and tickled her nose, grateful that her day was done.

IX.

"Get up, you."

"What the devil is she doing here?"

"She's sleeping. Take your time."

At a little after 4:00 in the morning, while drifting in a dream in which she toured the battlefields of Europe in a pair of English shoes, accompanied by Tuck and her grandmother, Estrella felt a pair of hands against her limbs and sat up to be blinded by a light. In the glare, she saw what looked like effigies ... or ghosts ... ghosts with heads like turtle shells. They were home guards, Carlitos on patrol.

They were dressed like English soldiers – but not like those in India or Egypt, who sported khaki drill and light slouch hats to keep their bodies cool. These fellows were colonials in an unimportant place, and as such were issued surplus kit from World War I – heavy olive wool designed to hold the body's heat.

So they were Carlitos, but Carlitos of a special kind – local whites – irregulars who'd volunteered for duty as they'd been raised to do. But their impulse wasn't bravery or valour, a matter of character. It was hormonal, part of an old, established cycle of blood ... the belief that it was better to stop a bullet than to give the people with the most to gain a taste of what it meant to organise and kill with guns.

"Hands up. Don't move. Are you deaf? I said don't move."

Estrella dipped and cowered with an arm above her brows to save her pupils from the light. When her eyes adjusted she observed that there were three.

"Declare your business," said the one who held the lantern. Another rubbed a billy club against his palm. The third one held a bolt action rifle with the muzzle pointing down.

Declare your business, she repeated to herself. What he really mean to say by that?

Although she spoke English, it was sometimes hard for her to understand official speech. The gun was frightening in itself, but it also made her think of Simón; and she stood stiffly, a nervous grin across her face, trying to look polite, wondering if her understanding was correct.

"Bloody insubordinate," the lantern bearer said. "She's trying to be difficult, and I'm running out of patience and time. I'm tired and I'm hot. The shift is almost done. Just make it simple. Lock her up."

"But I ain't do nothing wrong," Estrella said in disbelief. "Lock me up for what?"

"Well, declare your bloody business then," the lantern bearer said.

"But what you mean by that?"

The one who held the rifle leaned towards the lantern bearer's ear and said, "According to the proper regulations, you're supposed to ask her name and age and where she lives."

The lantern bearer shouted, "Who the hell put you in charge?"

"It's not about being in charge. It's about correct procedure. Is this how you'd interrogate a spy?"

"Which she is – obviously. Another German in disguise."

The one with the billy club began to laugh.

Now that is what you call a *boof*, Estrella thought. When he tell him that is like he stun him with a uppercut. Which part of me could be a spy? I thought it ain't have nobody who could *boof* like me. But I meet my match tonight.

"Are you mocking me, you little shit?" the lantern bearer asked.

The one who held the rifle stepped in front of Estrella to cut him off.

"Little darling," said the rifle holder, "what's your name? We're out on duty. There's a curfew going on. Do you understand me? Okay. Let me say it in *Sancoche*."

When she'd heard his explanation, she was irritated with herself. For her, the war was an important thing, and from what the rifleman had told her, she'd wasted their time.

"You're not allowed to sleep out here," he added. "Everybody must be off the street. If you want, we can give you a ride."

"I live real far from here, sir."

"How far?" the lantern bearer asked in English, stepping forward as he tugged the rifle holder to the rear.

"Way up in a far place, sir?"

The one with the billy club began to whisper to the rifleman, who sucked his teeth and tramped away.

"And what's that far place called?"

He brought the lantern close against her face so she could feel and smell the heat.

Carefully, she said, "That kind o' place, sir, ain't have no name."

"If you don't have a place to go," he told her in a change of voice, "I could arrange for you to have one for the night. I think a night would help you get over whatever's put you in this mood. What do you think? I could make that happen. Is that what you want?"

The subtlety had missed her, and she shrugged and said, "Okay."

He took her answer for a taunt and led her down the steps across the square, which had been puddled by the rain.

On the street, adjacent to the statue where Simón had left her, was a car, which in daylight would reveal itself to be a whitewalled Buick Century – silver, with a running board and bug-eyed headlamps on its elongated nose.

With the plush interior pressing on her back, Estrella felt relieved. Not a horse. Not a truck. But a fucking motorcar. On top o' that, a bed to sleep.

The lantern bearer sat behind the wheel and asked the one with the billy club to sit beside him. The rifle holder sat beside Estrella in the back. Someone pressed a button and a motor whirred the iron roof away, and Estrella sank with deep amazement in the toffee-coloured seat.

When they'd driven up and down the foreshore road, completing their patrol, she sat up suddenly and turned towards the rifleman and introduced herself in formal English: "I'm sorry. I'm Estrella. Nice to meet you. I didn't catch your name?"

He nodded, lit a cigarette and stuck it in his young, impassive face.

The driver tossed his head and ordered, "Stub that bloody light!"

The rifle holder answered, "Go to hell," and clamped the gun between his knees.

"You don't listen. That's your problem."

"Daddy, I'm a grown man with a family, for Jesus' sake. I'm not a child anymore."

The father tapped the shoulder of his younger son, who rode beside him.

"Your brother told me he's a grown man. What do you think of that? The words were his, not mine. A grown man who can't do a bloody thing. You would think a grown man raised by good parents would have his own car by now. It's his turn to do transportation on patrol and he shows up in his father-in-law's big American car, which he can't even drive because the steering wheel is on the other bloody side. You would think a grown man would be able to prevent his wife from running around like a common whore. You would think a grown man would stop having bastard tadpole children all over this bloody island without any practical means for their support. You would think a grown man who had strings pulled so he could get into Cambridge would have paid attention and come back to this place with some damn respect. So he fails at everything and you pull more strings, and he gets appointed head of one of the island's finest schools. But does he hold on to the job? No! He goes off to be some kind of artist, like a bloody fag. You would think a grown man would realise that you can't build a business or a future or respectability from painting like a fairy, or writing stupid books. Paint a house, for God's sake. Or be whatever you call the people who serve the books in the library ... those ill-tempered spinsters. You would think a grown man would, by now, have taken stock—"

"I get the point," the younger son objected. "People are different, Daddy. Everybody can't be the same. Will just needs a little bit of time."

They'd gone around the square and passed beneath the arch that opened on the Queens, and the six cylinders pulled them smoothly up the grade between the former mansions and the median with the flowers and the trees.

"*Time?*" the father shouted. "Who has a lot of that these days? None of us have time. Black Well is a mess. They rioted again. Over what, who bloody knows. We have no bloody coconuts. They've all got bloody blight. The frigging Germans just might win the war. And the Chinese and the Lebanese are so deceitful and underhanded, they're making wads of money trading while we sit on sugar that nobody wants, while we feed cows that can't bring you ten pounds at the abattoir."

"We're part Irish," said the older son, who'd just turned thirty-two. "Once upon a time we were new here too. But I know it's not the same. The rules have changed. Now *we're* the ones who make them."

"Trying to be sarcastic?"

"No. More along the lines of sardonic."

"The Lebanese are saints. Of course. Of course. But of course you know this. Your wife is one of them." He stopped the car and leaned across his seat. "Where is she now? Do you know? How do you know she hasn't left your house while you're out here risking life and limb for King and country? The little bitch. Knowing her, she's leaving footprints on your ceiling. Giggling in your bed."

The man who held the rifle wiped his face. The car began to move again.

Estrella couldn't see for certain, but she knew he'd wiped away some tears, and she felt obliged to take his hand and reassure him that he'd be okay, that she knew what it was like to hear that what you love is wrong and that your passions are just careless dreams, that she'd bought from Lebanese people and everything was nice, and that the Chinese them was nice ones too, and that a Chinese girl had helped her with her books ... that you had to be a bright, bright man to be headmaster, that you shouldn't listen when you family tried to put you down, 'cause that is all they do – try to give you bad eye and bad mouth and blight you ambition and bring down you will ... that if you wife is out o' order then is up to you to ask her why she always fooling round, 'cause woman ain't just wicked so ... they wicked when they feel that something wicked is the only thing that's left to do ... like how she, Estrella Thompson, had to pinch a little money when she had to buy a book because she ain't grow up with people who understand that books is things that people have to have.

I had to thief from them when I run away, because I need to get a start in life and they ain't want me reach nowhere. But they should see me now. In a motorcar ... in a motorcar like those that bring the fancy English ladies to La Sala ... see there, we just pass it now ... the place where I see the man send the woman the note that make her face turn red like blood.

91

Look at me now. Driving in that kind o' car. And look how the car just pulling smooth like them boat that have engine. And look how it feel nice when the breeze blowing right past my face. And look how my life turn interesting already, and I ain't fully even reach where I going yet ... and look now ... I just pass Salan's, where I going get my shoes.

Where you is, Grandma? And where you is, Big Tuck? Nowhere where nobody who have anything to think 'bout even care. A place that ain't even have no name. A place that even other fishermen refer to as "back so" or "over so" or "under the cliff". How somebody can be happy when they come from a place that ain't have no name?

But I have a name. My name is Estrella Roselyn Maria Eugenia Thompson, and you see how I black so? And you see how my foot bare so? Is white man driving me, though, like how black man drive them English ladies. And I take that as a sign.

When I go back and see my grandmother and Big Tuck, people going know my name, and they will hear other people call my name and they will want to say, "That's my granddaughter." But how you could bring yourself to say, "That's my granddaughter," when is you tell me to leave? When is you turn me out like Joseph in the Bible?

And when I think about it now, I wasn't going to really run away. But I have my pride. And when my own grandmother come to me and tell me I have to leave, and when none o' my friends come to me and say, "Here, take this sixpence that I saving up," or, "Don't worry, I talk to my mother and she say you could come stay by we," or, "I praying for you. I praying for you. If I was a big person I would put down my foot," I had to make a move.

And if some o' them had done that ... if some o' them had done what they bound to do as friends, then them evil people couldn't go on with their stupidness. They couldn't go on with their wickedness. They couldn't do something as ignorant, worthless, ungodly and savage like turning out a child.

I ain't plan to tell nobody I was going to leave. Because I wasn't going to leave. But they test my pride. They question my ambition. They put a dare to me.

But is jealous they jealous like Joseph brothers. And one day, one day – it might take awhile, but is sure to come – a blight going take this island, and they going have to come to Seville. And they going see me and ain't even know is me until I tell them. That is how much I going change.

"Mister, don't mind," she whispered to the rifleman beside her. She tapped his shoulder through the heavy wool. "Mister, don't you mind."

Without looking, he removed her hand and gently squeezed it with condolence. For her. For him. For history. For life.

"I'm sorry, miss," he muttered.

His father and his brother laughed.

"Is okay," she said. "Is awright."

At the governor's gate they made a left and took the rising stretch of road that led to an exclusive area called Savanna Ridge.

The governor's tall brick fence was on their right, and in the thinning darkness Estrella saw the shadow of the town becoming smaller, shrinking like a drought-afflicted lake. Out to sea, a golden razor sliced along the dark horizon.

She felt a nudge and looked at Will, the one beside her with the gun. He wrestled with a hook along his belt and handed her his water can. It was made of tin and dented, with a body like a wheel, and had a short, thick neck with a big, wide mouth. Around the neck there was a collar, with a chain that held the cap. And as Estrella tipped her head and sucked and gulped and swallowed, making loud barbaric sounds, the cap began to beat against the tin.

The water had a bad metallic taste, and on the rim there was the been-up-all-night odour of a soldier's mouth. But she drank it with a grateful throat, and sloshed it round her teeth and gums and heard its falling change in pitch as it began to fill her stomach, rising from a bellow to a gurgle that was shrill, like a spigot spewing beer into a mug.

"It have more, please?"

She used her sleeve to wipe her lips.

Will leaned against the seat in front of him.

"Are you finished with your water?"

His brother and father passed him their cans and he gave them to the girl, who began to drink in spurts, tossing back her head and guzzling, then pausing to breathe deeply and think.

Ahead of them she saw the fork that led along Savanna Ridge, whose lovely homes she knew from all the times she'd been sent by her grandmother with deliveries from the market – times at which she'd trotted up the Queens with trays of fish packed up in ice and wrapped in plantain leaves and sugar sacks balanced on her head, and idled by kitchen doors and gazed down at the grand savanna – an imposing sward behind the governor's house – while waiting to be paid.

When they came upon the fork, she thought they were taking her to one of these, a house that she imagined would be owned by one of them, because the owners of these houses on Savanna Ridge were white. She began to wonder if she'd ever seen their wives at La Sala; but she didn't linger on this thought, which faded quickly as she wondered how and where she'd sleep ... on a cot, perhaps, or on the floor ... or squeezed into a wicker chair out on the porch.

As if how and where she'd sleep had been decided, she began to think about the coming morning, when she planned to go to town to buy her shoes. And if she didn't have enough to buy an English pair, she thought, she'd buy whatever pair she could afford. Is not like the shoes would come with *England* stamp on it. And if *England* stamp on it, it must have something you could use to rub it off.

That decided, she began to see herself behind a house with a veranda as big as the deck of a ship, sitting in the grass and gazing through the mist at the savanna.

Her brows drew tight and wrinkled as she summoned all the details of the view – the little zoo and garden in the corner by the bridge across the Abuelito River ... in the centre, clouds reflecting off the pond, which was encircled by a ring of palms ... at the racetrack, Queen Victoria Park, grooms and jockeys exercising horses, wheeling them around the final bend and easing as they came into the straight, the trainers in the grandstand watching through field glasses ... beside the track, the cricket pitch, the Nelson Oval, where herons floated just above the grass like laundry, flopping on the stones that made a loop to mark the boundary line ... and above it all, the smooth, unbroken rise of Mt Diablo's cone ... and in its foothills, old estates.

If it was up to me, Estrella thought, the way I feeling now, there wouldn't be another sea. If is me alone in this world, I'd dry up every sea it have and put the fishes in another place ... like a river or a pond ... so it would still have fish to eat. But there wouldn't be a single piece for me. I ain't going eat fish or nothing from the sea no more. Only chicken and meat and goat. Chicken back and cow foot and goat head for me. I done with the sea. And when it dry up, if it have anybody who have somewhere far to go, they could build a train along the seabed where the water used to be. I ain't want to wake up and see no goddamn blue tomorrow morning. All I want to see is green.

When they continued up the hill and didn't take the branching road, a mood of apprehension fell upon the car. Unconsciously, Estrella placed a hand against the lock and scratched her feet against the mat, her instincts dulled by lack of sleep.

"I thought we was going to a place that have a bed," she said.

"Oh," the father answered, drumming on the wheel and glancing at his younger son. "They have beds there, don't they?"

"Where?" Estrella asked.

They didn't answer, and she crossed her arms and wondered what to do.

"Where we going?" she asked the one beside her, kneeling on the seat. "Why nobody ain't talking?" She put her hand against his shoulder. "Somebody talk to me."

With a heavy sigh he mumbled, "We're going up to Thunder Hill."

X.

It was a citadel constructed in the 1800s by the British on a ridge a thousand feet above the town. There were many buildings there. Among them were the prison and the island's only working fort.

"Will," she said in disbelief, sinking in her seat, "is there you really taking me?"

"Hold her," said the father.

Will looked at her and didn't move.

"Will, I gave you an order."

"Father, go to bloody hell."

"You!" he shouted at his younger son. "Get in the back right now."

"This is really stupid," said the younger son, who did as he was told.

I lose, Estrella thought. I lose. I fucking gamble and I lose. I ain't do nothing wrong. I ain't trouble nobody. And look how everything was going good. They even give me water and let me drink. They ask me if I want a ride. I say yes. They ask me if I want a bed. I say yes. Is because I laugh? They ain't still vex 'bout that? If is that, then I sorry. But it can't be that. Maybe they change they mind and think I is a spy for true. But a spy for who? Maybe they telling lie. Maybe they ain't even going where they say. Maybe they carrying me 'way to take advantage. I think is that you know. I think is that. In fact I *know* is that. I wonder if is that? What else they could want to do me but rape me off? 'Cause I ain't do nothing.

Calm yourself, Estrella. Calm yourself. Don't act like Pepper now. Is three o' them and one o' them is holding you. If you try to fight them with you body they will win. Play fool to catch the wise. Go on like you going to sleep. And when you feel his hand ease up then you bolt. One man take advantage already and you had the chance to use the knife. But what you do? You act like a fool.

Jesus Christ come off you cross and witness this today – if I get the chance again I ain't thinking what to do. I ain't *guessing* what to do. I *know* what I going do. I going jam them with this knife. And who dead – dead. And who live – live. Because I tired. Everything I touch is like I wrong. Everybody want to advantage me. From my grandmother and Big Tuck and them coolie people down by Speyside. Is what wrong with me so? Is what they see in me so make them think they could do that? Even Joseph. He nice and thing, but he just couldn't gimme a blasted ride without wanting to feel up my leg. And that Simón Bolívar. He's another thing. He going go down in history. I wonder if he know that? He going go down in history as the last fucking man who advantage me. Every rope have a end. And every hook have a point. And I at the end o' my hook right now. And somebody going get hurt.

Thunder Hill had always seemed foreboding to the girl. She'd seen it many times by boat and had always thought it had an evil look.

Up close it was larger than she'd thought. It was also not a single building, but many buildings carefully emplaced on different heights, and every level had a scheme of thick retaining walls – some of them as thick as seven feet.

After coiling upward with the walls for miles and passing many ruins on the slopes below, they parked on the parade ground, which was grassy, and in width and length a little smaller than a soccer field.

"You're not going to jail," Will said. He pointed to another building on an upper hill. "We're going over there."

There was the citadel, a massive installation with an inner courtyard large enough to hold five thousand troops. It was sunk into the hill and surrounded by a trench, which had made it hard to hit in the colonial wars. Apart from the prison, it was the only portion of the complex that was still in use, and below the ramp that led towards it they could see platoons of US soldiers doing callisthenics on a grassy rise.

"Daddy, why're we stopping?" asked the younger son, annoyed.

The father answered, "Just to let her walk."

"With all due respect, Daddy, I don't have time for this. We're the last ones back, I'm sure. We should've been here hours ago. You and Will can sort this out. Let's go."

The father cleared his throat and put the car in gear, and they drove along a ramp towards the citadel. At the gate, the father mumbled, "Rawle."

On hearing this, the guard, who'd come on duty after they'd gone on their patrol, saluted them although they wore no signs of rank, and begged them for a chance to wash the car.

Inside, they parked adjacent to a line of trucks and armoured cars. The cars had cannons and machine guns sticking out.

Estrella's real hope as she saw it was the diver. Would he remember her? After all this time? And if he did, would he talk on her behalf? Was he one of the men out there in undershirts and trousers exercising?

She was standing with her back against the car, and her detainers faced her in a semicircle, touching-length away. Their faces had expressions that she couldn't read.

"So, smarty," said the father, taking off his helmet, which he clamped under his arm, "what should we do with you now?"

He was tired, and he shook his head to make himself alert. Like his sons, who'd taken off their helmets too, his hair was blond with streaks of sandy brown.

"I have a friend," she said. "A soldier man who do man hoovers in the sea ..."

As she spoke, she slyly watched the gate. From here to there, she estimated, was a hundred yards. She also paid attention to their stance, how they moved their weight, how sometimes they'd lean apart to stretch or gesture, creating gaps, tempting her to drop her head and run. And each time she thought of this but waited for a better time, her desperation grew, and she felt the urge to bet her life as would a gambler in the hole.

If I just run just like so, they could just shoot me, she thought. And I'd be too far to fight them with my knife. But if I have that gun, I could protect myself ... and if that guard boy who salute them try to stop me, I would shoot that fucker too. I would shoot every last fucking one o' them. Whatever amount o' bullet it could have in that gun ... how I feeling now ... I ain't 'fraid to use it.

Dawn was beginning to break by now and Estrella had an understanding of each face. Will, the older son, who was in his early thirties, had clear blue eyes. The father had a slim moustache. The younger son had freckles and a dimple in his chin. They were all of average build, and she could see from their faces that their heavy uniforms gave them added stock; but from their eyes, which were fatigued, she perceived them to be worn, and doubted that they'd have the strength to give pursuit.

"What's your name again?" the older brother asked.

He leaned against the gun as if it were a walking stick, with the stock against the damp stone floor.

"Estrella," she said, blinking sleep out of her eyes. "I told you once before."

His body heaved, his mouth opened, then he stopped. He did this five more times, heaving then stopping, like a discus thrower warming up. Then finally, as everybody stared at him, he let it go.

"Look," he said, embarrassed, "just get out of here. Go home."

She began to walk in circles. The sudden shift in circumstances was a lot for her to bear, the lack of plot disorienting. There was no clear pattern. No clear link between action and reaction. Cause and effect. It didn't feel like life.

"Just go home just like so?" she asked when she was settled.

He shook his head, excused himself, and yawned.

"So what all this was about?" she asked, looking at each man in turn. "You must have a reason why you do me what you do."

The father said, "One day it will soak in."

She shrugged and thought, One day in truth, but not right now. I ain't want to talk no more. I ain't care 'bout nothing no more. I just want to go my way and never see these people face again.

"So how I get back to town from here?" she asked.

They looked at her in silence. They hadn't thought that far.

"If I have to walk then I have to walk," she said, holding back her rage. Then speaking in a clear, respectful tone, she asked, "Well, may I kindly have my things?"

They craned their necks and cocked their heads, confused.

"What things?" the father asked.

"That I bring from home." Her brows and voice were raised. "My basket with my blanket and my books ... my clothes ... my dolly ... my soap ..."

The father turned towards the younger son, the one with the freckled face, raised his hands indifferently, and shrugged.

"Sir, where are my things?" Estrella asked again. She rolled her fists and bit her lips, squeezing back the other words.

The father answered, "Must be where you left them, I suppose."

"Sir, you is the one who told me I had to come. Not that I want to make a big thing out o' this. But when you hold my arm and told me to come on and you bring me to the car, I think one o' you was going bring my basket. You leave it? You sure? I ain't mean to take up you time, but we could look in the car?"

She began to walk around the Buick, peering inside. They watched as if inebriated by a cocktail mix of indifference, regret and surprise, brows half-raised ... skin softly tingling from a mild attack of nerves ... something fearful, but not quite paranoia, an awareness that they might have hounded her too much, had crossed a line and entered a place they didn't understand and were therefore not equipped to rule.

"They were not my things," the father pointed out. "They were yours. What? Am I supposed to be your servant now? Same thing down at Speyside. Nobody wants to work on this damn island anymore. Everything is on the boss. *Boss do this. Boss do that.* Well, boss is tired now and boss wants to go home."

"You know all my money is in there, sir?" she droned, astounded by the loss. "I had it in my pocket but I move it. I wrap it up and put it in my basket right under my head in case it drop out o' my pocket in the night. You know all my clothes in there, sir? You know if I ain't get back my things I don't have nothing in this world, sir? When you answer me the way you answer me ... as if I ain't really lose nothing ... like this is a simple thing ... you did know how much it had in there, sir?"

"I was only doing my job," he said glibly. "You weren't supposed to be there. If you had obeyed the law, then none of this would have happened."

Desperate, Estrella trampled her pride and went down on one knee. "I begging you for a drive into town to get my things, sir. Please, sir, before somebody take away my things. I didn't mean to talk fresh, sir. I didn't mean to offend you, sir. Sometimes I can get carried away, sir, and talk like I don't have no sense or no upbringing, sir. But I'm not a hooligan or virago, sir. Please, can you carry me so I can go and get my things?"

"No, I can't," replied the man who owned the truck that had taken her from the bridge across the island to the Caribbean coast. "Carry you? I'm off duty now. But you're free to go on your own. The lesson has been learned. That's what's most important. The lesson has been learned."

Through the open gates of the gigantic fort, the broken-hearted girl could see the eastern sky becoming filled with shades of red. She thought she heard a creaking as her heart began to fall.

Dazed, she made a step towards the men, half-expecting them to tell her not to move.

"I ain't know what to say no more," she said, using her hands to part them. "But what you do to me is a sin. I will take this lesson to my grave. It have some wicked people in this world."

And as the father forced himself to laugh so he could drown his feelings of regret, Estrella Thompson ran towards the morning on her blisters, hoping that the one who held the gun would raise it, aim it and draw a breath, ensuring that the bullet that would free her from this life would hit her clean between the shoulder blades. This way she'd return to the cove in a coffin instead of in disgrace.

XI.

St William Rawle – the older son – was driving down the hill. The car was big, and the road was small, with many twisting turns, so with the steering wheel on what Carlitos called "the other side" he found it hard to judge the curves, forcing him to stop at every corner just to calculate the angle of the bends. Sometimes he stepped outside the car to look.

Considered from an unexpected point of view, the turns made him feel disoriented, made him question where he sat. In this way they called to mind the girl.

The last time he'd felt this way was when he'd first encountered Graham Greene's *The Power and the Glory*, and had felt a sense of urgency to write about someone as complicated as the whisky priest.

Compassion, he'd thought. That's what writing is about – compassion for the people on "the other side". And that's no easy thing to do. So, he'd written and still wrote – without support or glory – publishing his efforts at his own expense.

It was hot, and he'd raised the roof to shield him from the sun, and was using a yellow handkerchief to dab his neck as he perspired in his crushed white suit.

Alone in the car – his father and brother had been chauffeured home in the family Jag – he left the main road after passing the parade ground and drove along a lower rampart that led him to the wide, stone deck of a bastion.

The mighty stones had fallen over time. What was left recalled a lower jaw with blackened teeth, and he could see the footprints of the various buildings that had crumbled – barracks, cisterns, storage rooms.

The bastion had been built like an arrow, a hundred-metre flying wedge, lined on either side with cannons, some of which remained.

He wandered through the ruins in deep contemplation and went inside the old munitions building, which was larger than a parish church. It was cool and shaded there and he sat against a window ledge and thought about the girl, the whiteness of his suit intense against the grey volcanic stone and beautiful against the ocean blue that filled the empty arches of the missing doors.

He knew the girl, he thought. He knew her without knowing. But he'd like to know her more.

When he was headmaster he'd meet this kind of girl.

You'd be in your office on a Monday morning and one of your father's cronies – some member of the opera society or the yacht club, or some member of some board – would bring her in and introduce her as a Christian girl with sense and morals who deserved a chance, and you'd look at him and think, Okay, you've got an outside daughter and you went to church and got a case of guilt. Or if she's not your daughter, she's the object of some kind of complicated love. And you'd do what you could – which was a hell of a lot – and the girl would get in.

But these were not the circumstances of this girl ... Estrella. She didn't think in English, but she spoke the kind we speak here fairly well – which tells you that she's been to school, but not for many years. If she'd gone to school for longer, her English vowels wouldn't be so short, or as she'd say it, "shot".

She could be a farm girl though. She had that kind of ruggedness and strength. But if she were a farm girl her hands would be rough in a different way. No ... she didn't farm. She fished.

When you held her hand, or when she held yours, you were so stunned by the feeling that infused you – you don't even remember what happened. Only that she made you feel good ... so good that for the rest of the ride you found it hard to talk. You know what farm girls feel like. No, she isn't one of them. Her calluses ran in a line along the inside of her thumbs to where they joined the fullness of her hand, and you could feel them climbing like a set of rungs on the outside of her pointer. You got those kinds of calluses from pulling on a line. No ... she didn't farm. She didn't farm at all. She fished.

So Estrella is a fishing girl. By her voice, probably from down the wild Atlantic coast. She hadn't been in town for very long, because word would have come to you. And she surely didn't live in Black Well, where you went to find the young *negritas* you pay to pose for you so you can paint them in the nude.

This is such a funny backward island, this damn San Carlos place. It's okay to get young girls to stand around for hours in the flesh. But tell somebody you want to write and paint for the rest of your life and they think you need a weekend in a padded room.

But what is really strange is that this girl was sleeping in the street. Why would she have to do that? What could she have done? You get the sense that she's a warm and loving soul. What did she do?

Your family is your pride. You're nothing if you're not your blood. If someone kicks you out, you just go somewhere else. A relative. A friend. Or you stay and make amends. Because to leave your household is a big disgrace. And *you* know this very well. Because your wife just told you she wants a damn divorce and that's why you're here, marking time. You don't want to go home.

He walked outside across the flat expanse of stone, and stood there in the open, thinking of Rebecca ... Rebecca Salan ... Rebecca Salan his wife, then walked towards the point at which the walls converged into a prow, and saw the land below him sheer away.

On the lower slopes, the lines of other ruins and the edges of the sweeping thick retaining walls were overlapping like the kind of waves that cause an undertow, and St William Rawle, who'd gone away to Cambridge in the years before the war and flunked out in disgrace, put his hands behind his back and dropped his chin, sorry, lonely, and ashamed – at thirty-two, the unevacuated captain of a ship wrecked on a reef – and thought about his wife and wondered what had happened to the girl.

After she'd run away he'd argued with his father, who insisted that he'd actually been nice. His younger brother listened, but he didn't intervene, and only talked about it when their father went to change.

"Will, we know he's an ass."

They were moving through the courtyard to the storeroom with their weapons and their clothes. "But you've got to understand ... he's disappointed."

"Albert, what he did was wrong!"

"True, but in a way she brought it on herself."

"How?"

"Insubordination. If you let them get away with that, there's nothing left."

"Insubordination? She was frightened. She's a simple country girl."

"Don't get too high-minded now. You've screwed a lot of them."

"Why're we straying from the point?"

"But that *is* the point. You want to screw this girl, so you're getting sentimental."

"You're getting out of order now. Please stop it."

"Everybody likes to burn a little diesel now and then, but you've let this crossing over rule your life. What's this painting all about? Have you ever sold or shown a painting of a naked behind?"

"You just don't understand."

"Well ..."

"Albert Rawle, you *are* your father's child."

"That's good. He gets respect."

"No. He gets fear and hate."

"Listen, Will, and listen good. England is at war. There's a madman in Berlin. There's an emperor in Japan who thinks he's God on earth. There are brutes in Italy and Spain who think their backward countries have a reason to exist beyond their women and their wine. And you want me to waste time on a spat about a girl I hardly fucking know? Go home to Rebecca. Whatever she might be, she's your wife. Do you hear me? Get some sleep. In the morning everything will be okay. Drive safely. Everything is dodgy from the other side."

XII.

As St William contemplated all these things, Estrella watched him from the shadow of a ruined barrack on a grassy ramp of earth, the length of her against the ground, her knife sideways across her mouth, stalking.

When they didn't shoot her, she'd sped along the ramp and veered across the grass away from where she'd seen the Yankee soldiers, taking refuge in a crumbled building where she hid and watched the fort to see if she was being pursued. After thirty nervous minutes, she began to execute her slow escape, moving down the hill on trails, staying off the main.

She was hiding in the bushes when she saw the car, and at first she wasn't going to give pursuit. But when she realised that the one who had the gun was now alone, an idea came to mind.

It might not have come to mind if she'd seen one of the other two, but St William's timid driving made her think of him as soft. He sat close against the wheel and craned his neck across the dash; and observing this, and thinking of the way that almost everything he'd said was overruled, she chose him as the object of a lesson in revenge.

At one point she was sure he'd seen her – when she tried to dash across the road before he came around a bend. But he was focused on his inner life and didn't notice when she spun around and dived into the bush.

Lying on her side, she'd said, while watching him go by: "You would die in war in Europe. You're so careless and so soft." As soon as she'd said this, an image came to mind, an image that was instantly translated to a thought. It was an image of a knife against a throat, which was translated as, *I have to get him in the car*. After that there were no other thoughts. Just actions. Running. Hiding. Jumping. Rolling. Scaling. Shunting. Creeping. Crawling. Darting ... until now.

She watched him walking back and forth across the lonely open deck. Two truckloads of soldiers rumbled down the hill. If I going to do it then I have to do it now, she thought.

That man ain't going stand up there all morning. Any minute now he going go 'bout his business. And if he goes before you do what you suppose to do, then you plan get spoil.

If he could just frighten, she thought, as she disciplined her nerves. If he could just frighten when he come and see me in the car, and don't try to wrestle ... then it would be awright. Because as I lying here I ain't want to cut nobody anymore. Them things easy to think 'bout, but they hard to do unless you have them kind o' mind. And I ain't have them kind o' mind.

I have it sometimes, but I ain't have it right now. That's why it ain't good to talk out you intentions, even to yourself. 'Cause if you talk them is like you do them already, and you ain't going have the feeling to do them again.

Is like when somebody tell you the last part of a joke. You ain't bother want to hear the joke again. You know the whole joke now. Same way, I lie down here thinking what I going do, and now I ain't feel to do it.

I want to do it, but I ain't *feel* to do it. And that is two different things. Is like when a person want you do something, and you want to do it just because that person ask you, especially when they ask you in a forcing way.

Well, something inside me *want* me to do this thing. Want me to shuffle down this hillside and hide in that car and jump up when that man pull that door and drag him by the arm inside and tell him, "Shut you mouth. Shut you mouth. Shut you goddamn mouth and listen to me right now before I open up you fucking gills and gut you. I going take you for a ride just like how you take me for a ride. I going take you out o' you way and mash up whatever business you have, just like how you mash up mine. How that feel now? How that feel? This is what you going do. You going take me back where you find me so I can find my things. And just in case we don't find it, you going have to gimme a hundred ... no ... a thousand pounds as pay for what I lose and for how much you make me go through. For all the suffer I suffer. For all the pain I feel. And as a matter o' fact, gimme that money right now 'cause I ain't trust you. I ain't trust you at all. I use to trust you one time. But I ain't trust you again. You grow up and hear all kind o' thing 'bout all kind o' people how they thief. But nobody ever tell you white man thief too. You hear how everybody thief. And they always say we nigger is the worst. And I myself use to think so too. But I see for myself now. All man is man. All flesh is flesh. Drive this fucking car right now and drive it fast. I lose too much time already. I have a lot o' catching up to do. You ain't going hold me back no more."

That's what I *want* to do, she thought. But that ain't what I *feel* to do. Maybe I is a coward or something. But that ain't what I feel to do. And I ain't really know what I feel to do. All I know is I want back my things and my money. And I ain't want to fuss no more.

Her head was heavy with combusting thoughts. The heat was as solid as a piston pumping downward in its case. She stood up as St William Rawle began to move towards the car.

Something was about to happen. What, she wasn't sure. And she felt it was important to look at her surroundings as if she might be seeing them for the final time.

Down the coast and to her left she noticed the hooking headlands of the harbour in Seville, but a spur came angling down across her line of sight and she couldn't see the town. In the sky, beyond the spur, there was a stack of piling clouds. It would rain.

It would rain. But she would have known this even if she hadn't seen the clouds. She would have known this even if she'd only seen the water, which was frilled with waves, or if she'd simply closed her eyes and concentrated as she breathed, for as a daughter of the sea she'd learned to smell the rain from miles away, like a shark was born to catch the faintest scent of blood.

A voice said, "Hey."

She withdrew behind the column with her back against the stone.

"Hey."

She put away the knife. The voice had been hers.

"Who's there?" St William called.

From her hiding place, she saw him tilt his head.

"Come," she said.

"Who's there?"

"I say come."

"Come where?"

"Up here."

He put his hands against his hips.

"Is it who I think it is?"

"I can't read you mind."

"Is it ... is it you?"

"Is me ... yes ... is me."

He pointed at the ramp.

"What are you doing there?"

"I don't know."

"Well ... what do you want?"

She swallowed.

"I don't know. Just come."

"There's no one here. Just me. They're gone."

"I know."

"So you come then."

"Why I should come to you?"

"Well ... let's see ... the ramp is very steep."

She sucked her teeth and thought, I ain't able for this *rass* right now.

"You know what? Just forget it. Just go you way. I ain't want no worries no more."

"I don't want trouble either. If you want, let's talk."

"Where?"

He looked around and dabbed his brows.

"Let's do it in the car."

She drummed her fingers on the wall.

"No. If you want to talk to me, you have to come up here."

He was too far away for her to hear his footsteps growing closer, but near enough for her to hear his leather Oxfords crunching dirt and gravel on the crumbling stone.

In the middle of the floor there was a pool where rain had settled. She went to wash her feet and saw reflections of her face and thought, You ain't look like nothing, and you have to look like something when you meet this man. He have to look at you and judge you as a person that is talking sense. And he ain't going hear what you saying proper if you looking like a tramp.

Yesterday you look like something. When you bathe off and you was riding in the back o' Joseph truck, every man was looking hard. Now you look like chew-up-and-spit-out. Who would find you interesting now? Who would give you a job? You could go to the Chinese shop and beg a little alms from the girl who help you with you books. But where you would go from there? Back to you grandmother and Big Tuck and plead with them to take you in ... looking mash-up so, and ragged so, and smelling so? So they could ask you what you was doing and what happen to the things you leave with? Eh-eh, you gone with high pride and big ambition and come right back with two long hands like ... *Rawle!*

The skin along her body prickled when it struck her that the man she was about to talk to was the one who'd gone away to England and returned with two long hands, the legendary failure invoked by Big Tuck.

She could hear the forward motion of his footsteps now, and with a greater urgency began to slap the dirt out of her clothes.

Tuck might be a wicked fucker, but this time I taking what he say, 'cause I hear the father cuss him 'bout the same damn thing ... how he gone to big school in England and ain't come back with nought. Well, is a good thing you never stick him with you knife, because now you have a better chance to get what you want. Because that man brain ain't sharp like yours. You could outbrain him. He's a dunce.

Don't care how he was headmaster. The man is a blasted dunce. His own father say so. And no dunce man going outbrain me. I going talk to him like a barrister. I going make my case. And if he is a soldier man or a policeman or whatever he suppose to be, then he suppose to know the law. And I read 'bout them big barrister how they persecute they case when people thief and dirty other people name. And I hear it on the rediffusion box as well. Well, if this dunce man is the law then I going persecute my case against him and win. 'Cause what they do me wasn't right.

They take advantage. And I tired o' people taking advantage o' me. Because o' people taking advantage why I ain't wearing my shoes now and going about the place to find my job. And no way under the sun that could be right.

She spat into her hands and smoothed her hair and scooped it into a bun while she used one foot to scrub the other in the dirty pool. Deciding that her clothes were too filthy, she turned them inside out. The colours on the inside had a richer tone. They were not as badly bleached. And she rolled her cuffs above her elbow and swung out from behind the column – as solid in her presence as a door.

"Mr Rawle," she said in her most formal English, swinging her right arm like a baseball pitcher warming up, "I need to speak with you."

He paused along the ramp, some thirty yards away, and pushed his hat off his sweating brow, leaning with his arms on his forward knee, frozen in a stride.

"Mr Rawle," Estrella called again. She raised her voice and placed her hands against her hips. "Mr Rawle, you need to come right now. I need to talk to you."

The seams that lined her face from mouth to cheek were pulsing as she walked, and when her shadow striped St William's back and shoulders from above, he looked away and winced as if he thought he would be caned. This unleashed a brutal instinct from Estrella's core, urging her to hook him in the collarbone, and use his hat to slap his face and give him what the British called "a proper straightening out".

"Mr Rawle," she said. "I come to talk to you because – as a soldier man or policeman or whatever kind o' man you is – you is the law. My name as I told you before is Estrella Thompson, and I have come to persecute my case in front o' you. Yesterday afternoon I left my home to come to town to buy a pair o' shoes because I want to get a decent job so I could improve myself in life. I will be honest with you – my grandparents put me out. They are ignorant people. They don't want to learn and they don't want me to learn, and I want to learn. And because I want to learn, it cause a problem. Because I like to read, the people I live with stop talking to me. Even my own blood. So I left my house and went to sleep in a old canoe. Then the people on my beach began to say I'm the reason why fish stop coming. I took a bus to come to town and by accident I took the wrong bus, which drop me off in Speyside. And after I waited for a long time I began to walk until I got a lift in a truck. I began to walk again until I got a ride from a man on a horse. I came off downtown right by the statue, but then the rain began to fall and I went in the park. The rain came more so I left the park to sleep by the building. And then you came and saw me and thought I was a troublemaker. Mr Rawle, I am not making any trouble, sir. I am not like the people from Black Well that I heard you father saying make a lot o' trouble all the time. I am not the best girl. But everybody have faults. My head is good and I want to be something in life. Now, as I told you before – that bag I had with me had all my belongings in this world, including all my money. I have no money now, sir. Not a penny in the world. Which simply means I cannot go home."

As she looked at him, awaiting his response, he closed each eye to look at her from slightly different angles, and saw that one of his suspicions had been right – her face had perfect lines. If you halved it right along her nose, and took away the crescent scar, the sides were exactly the same. No part of it was deviated, or uneven, or of a different height.

"We were wrong," he said, exhaling, "but there is nothing I can do."

"I'm not asking you for money, sir. I need a ride go to town."

She slipped her hands inside her pockets.

At least you'll clear your chest, he thought. Do this thing and then it will be over. You'll never have to see her for the rest of your life.

XIII.

They drove in an electric silence. Between them was a soundless hum until she asked, when they'd passed the last retaining wall that led to Thunder Hill: "You think what you do me could be right?"

"It's not a matter of right and wrong," he told her, slowing as they came upon a curve.

"Is just wrong," she said.

Her arms were crossed; her back against the door.

"It's not as simple as that. It's not a simple thing at all."

"You reached all the way to headmaster. I've never been to school. Explain me what you mean."

"We're all faced with hard choices every day," he said with reservation. "And sometimes doing one thing for right will make you to do another thing for wrong. I always try to do the right thing. But sometimes in doing the right thing people get hurt. It has nothing to do with you."

"I'm very disappointed, Mr Rawle. You don't know how disappointed I am. Stop the car and let me out."

They had got to the place where she could see the turnoff to Savanna Ridge, the place she'd thought they were going to take her. The memory lit again the fire under what was now a third degree of pain.

In the tense, unmoving car she looked away from him towards the sea, and held her stomach as she felt the mass of something dark and sleek inside her rushing upward from her depths, driving with the power of a whale. She held the dashboard and addressed him quickly, rushing all her words before the monster whooshed out, making waves, at which point words wouldn't matter anymore.

"Mr Rawle," she told him in *Sancoche*, "the way I heard you father curse you is just how my grandmother curse me. When I see you wipe you face in the back o' this same car here I feel so sorry for you, because I know the pain you was feeling in you heart, because I feel that same pain too ... anger, shame and heartbreak knot up in one. And when I tell you I vex with my grandmother and grandfather, you know, Mr Rawle, believe me. I vex. But I can't vex with you. You ain't owe me nothing. Them is my grandmother and my grandfather. You ain't owe me nothing. But truthfully, Mr Rawle, you make me lose my faith. I use to think all I had to do was try, that all I had to do was give it everything and the rest would just be ambition and luck. I born unlucky. But ambition is not something you can have by yourself. Other people have to have it for you too. Because if they ain't want you to be nothing, and if they ain't give you a chance to be nothing, nothing going come of you. You teach me something, headmaster. You teach me a lesson I will keep in my head all my life. You know what? It don't even make sense I go for my basket now. That basket must be gone."

With this, she pushed against the door and sprinted down the road, and when she reached the spot at which Savanna Ridge branched off to her left and she could see the loop of whitewashed stones around the cricket ground and the flutter of royal palms around the pond, she drew the knife and flung it in the bush and howled.

After this, she straightened up and walked again.

Mingled with the mist of sound suspended in the air above Seville she heard the slapping of her blistered feet against the rain-slick road and the drumming of blood inside her ears.

Is a fifty-minute walk to the market, she thought, and it have people there I could ask for something, a little money, a little water, a little *choops* o' food to eat.

You granny ain't suppose to come to town for days, and although them market people bound to know you people blame you for the fishing blight, they ain't going know yet that they turn you out.

But what they going think when they see you with you clothes turn inside out, and smell you sour breath and hear the failure in you voice? They going want to know. And what hide in darkness must come out to light. So even if you ain't going tell them, in time they bound to know.

She was deep in these thoughts and about to cross the road and take the Queens towards the harbour from the governor's gate, when she saw a movement from the corner of her eye and skipped up on the verge.

With the steering of the Buick on "the other side," St William's face was just a foot away. Speaking in *Sancoche*, he said, "You ain't even know you size I'm sure."

His eyes were red as if he'd been crying, and his nostrils quivered when he tried to stop his running nose.

"I ain't wear no shoes before," she told him curtly and began to walk again.

He caught up to her and stopped again as horns began to honk and other drivers cursed and ordered him to move.

Standing on the grassy verge, Estrella leaned against the car, put her elbows on the roof, and waved the cars behind him to go on. With her belly inches from his face, he stole a little of her musty smell, and feeling sentimental, wished to God that human beings were born with special pockets in the nose for keeping special scents.

When the cars had passed, she crossed the street. He scrambled from the vehicle and chased her, and she felt a secret pleasure when she heard his footsteps coming close.

"My wife have a lot o' shoes at home," he said, and took her by the arm. "Dress too. Blouse too. Skirt too. And I sure she have

119

too much o' anything a girl like you might want. You were right. You *are* right. What we did was wrong."

"Thank you, Mr Rawle," she said, twisting from his grasp. "But I want you look at me and look at me good."

"Okay ..."

"I ain't come to town to beg no alms. I come to get a job. And I might be doing the wrongest thing in the world, but I going ask you a favour. And if you can't do it, you should tell me you can't do it. Don't make no false promise to me."

"Okay ..."

With a smile, she said in English, "Fuck off and leave me alone."

"What?"

"I came to town to get a job, Mr Rawle. I didn't come to ask for charity from the likes o' you."

"You want a work?" he shouted as he grabbed her blouse.

"Let me go," she said between her teeth. "Let me go. You better fucking let me go."

She seized him by the neck and they began to grapple, breathing hotly in each other's faces till he used his tennis grip to twist her arm, which made her lose her balance, and she fell.

"If you want a job, then ask," he said, while pinning her down. "Who the fuck you think you are?"

She spat at him and freed a hand and reached into her pocket. But the fucking knife was gone.

From all angles, people rushed towards them, and he stood and waved them off. They hushed but didn't move. They wanted to observe the drama as it turned.

"Just who do you think you are?" he shouted as he rose. "Tell me. Tell me now!"

He stood there feeling helpless but it came across as rage. The girl had spat his compassion in his face. And he needed her to see him as he knew himself to be – a man who wanted her to live in a different island from the one in which they lived today, a Mr Rawle who was nothing like his father.

"I ain't going beg you for a thing," Estrella said when she was on her feet.

"You can cook?" he asked.

She brushed the grit from her elbows and watched his blue eyes.

"All poor people can do them things."

"You can cook?" he asked again, glancing at his dirty clothes.

"Anything you want. Except fish."

"And clean?"

"*That* and wash and press."

Two policemen jostled through the crowd. St William told them all was well. After making whispered enquiries they left him with the girl.

"And if you want," he said, avoiding what he thought of as her *damn man-breaking stare*, "you could live in. It's a big place. You could have your own room."

Chewing on her pride, she told him, "But I'd need to start today."

"You can."

"And I'd like to start right now before anything else happen and nothing don't work out."

"You can start when we get home."

When they reached the car, she asked him, "Could you teach me how to read and write proper? Even if you take it from my pay?"

He shook his head and offered her a Dunhill. She took it and they smoked.

When they'd begun to drive again, he took the road that led along the big savanna, and she looked out at the horses exercising on the track, their sharp hooves lifting dirt, and up above, the lovely houses on the ridge. Then St William turned onto an avenue that led away from all of this.

They passed some newer houses, even larger than the ones along the rise, and they privately acknowledged in their separate ways that something had been started when they grappled, something that would complicate their lives.

"Wake me when we reach," she said, and closed her slanted eyes. "I going catch some sleep."

She hadn't fallen fully into sleep when she began to feel the vehicle slowing down. When it stopped, she sat up lazily, awakened by the sound of conversation. Beside St William's window was a man. Grazing on the verge, there was a horse.

"Who's that?" she asked him when the car began to move again, although she knew the answer by the rider's voice and smell. He'd tipped his hat politely, but it didn't seem as if he knew her; but she knew him by his scent. He smelled of rum, cedar shavings and carbolic soap, but none of them intensely – and also, she believed, a little bit of her.

He was red like new pottery, with a long straight nose, and his tight cream pants were stained with grass and dirt.

"That's Wilfredo Dominguez," said St William tightly, "and he's coming from my house. My wife is there. You'll meet her. My little son as well. Wilfredo is the finest carpenter you'll ever meet. In fact he made our matrimonial bed."

"I'm glad to know his name."

"Are you okay?"

"No, sir, I'm not okay at all."

"What's the matter?"

She closed her eyes, hoping to reclaim the peace of sleep.

"I ain't want to wear you wife old shoes, Mr Rawle. I walk too far from country for that. I need a ride to Salan's. I need to buy my own."

"I thought you didn't have any money."

"I lost it. But is *your* fault, so you going have to give me back fourteen pounds and fifty pence." Then she remembered the money from Wilfredo, whom she thought of as Simón. "Plus twenty pounds on that."

"That's a lot."

"That's my point."

"I don't know if I have that."

"If you ain't have it, put me out."

"Okay. You'll get it when we're home."

"Good. As soon as we get the money we going to Salan's."

"Well, you can't go there like that. Maybe you should wait until you've had a bath and tried on something you could wear."

"No, sir. I ain't have that kind o' time."

"Well, I can't go like this. And to get there you'll need a car."

She touched his shoulder.

"Listen me now, and listen me good. When we bathe and change our clothes, we going out."

Afterword
Russell Banks

We don't see it attempted much these days, perhaps because American writers (and readers) are so blinded by standard-issue realism on the one side and escapist fantasy on the other, but Colin Channer's *The Girl with the Golden Shoes* is a nearly perfect moral fable. It's an ancient, essentially European literary form, the moral fable; but think of Hemingway's *The Old Man and the Sea* or Thornton Wilder's *The Bridge of San Luis Rey*. Think of Faulkner's *The Bear* or Stephen Crane's *The Red Badge of Courage*. Those are the modern American classics in the form. A more recent example is Cormac McCarthy's *The Road*. Like them, *The Girl with the Golden Shoes* is a short narrative, shorter than a conventionally realistic novel, that is, but not so short as to be confused with a mere story. Like them, it's set more or less outside of present time, yet is not meant to be read as historical fiction, and happens in a place that's slightly outside the known or at least the familiar world. Even the title, *The Girl with the Golden Shoes*, calls to mind those old fables and fairy tales, pre-Christian European folk tales and medieval romances.

The protagonist is individualised, yes, a recognisable Afro-Caribbean country girl of the early 1940s born and raised on a recognisable Caribbean island that's a little like Cuba, a little like Jamaica, and a little like Hispaniola or Trinidad, yet none of the above. She's a spunky, intelligent girl named Estrella – ah, yes, the star – poised at the exact end of childhood and the exact beginning of adulthood. But she's from a world that does not recognise adolescence; that is to say, a world way older than ours, in which there are children and there are adults and nothing in between; and thus, of necessity, she seems flattened somewhat, a premodern "type" – or better yet, an archetype. Estrella is the archetype of the innocent provincial youth who one day sets out for the big city, here called Seville, to find her fortune and her fate. To become somebody. It's usually a boy on this journey, rarely a girl, but Channer knows that archetypes are gender-blind. And given his tripartite theme of dependency, trust and betrayal (about which, more later), it's a more intriguing tale morally if it's about a girl. She's adopted, sort of, raised by her grandparents, which is to say she's a child without real parents, a foundling without a binding self-defining family, making it necessary for her to locate her true identity outside the family, to find it even, as is typical, outside the community she's been raised in. For the community has cast her out. The reason being – again, typically – she's the solitary bearer of a curse, the unintentional cause of widespread, otherwise inexplicable suffering in her village. This makes her an exile, a wanderer who can't go home again. Condemned to travel the open road, she will be tested and tempted, and the tests and temptations will create her character, which, by the end of her tale, will be different than it was at the beginning. By the end, no longer a child, no longer innocent or naive, after many trials and tribulations, Estrella will have arrived at adulthood, wise and walking in a state of grace that is apparent to all who meet her there. Still dependent (she's a black woman, after all, and this is a racialised society, and sexist); but no longer trusting. She's protected therefore against betrayal and thus is able to place a wholly legitimate claim on those emblematic golden shoes. It's *Cinderella* and *Sleeping Beauty* and *The Frog Prince* all rolled into one, with a little Huckleberry Finn and Tom Jones thrown in for good measure.

Well, it's all fine and dandy, all well and good, to admire the ease and intelligence with which Colin Channer has engaged the ancient and honourable, essentially European tradition of the moral fable, and important to praise the way he's introduced into it elements that are native to the Caribbean archipelago and therefore to the African diaspora, bringing it up to date and speed, as it were, and in the process reinvigorating it. He's creolised the form, given it a strictly New World DNA without cutting off its Old World roots. That alone is an extraordinary achievement. But we ought also to admire the apparent ease and intelligence with which he has addressed a modern (actually a postmodern, postcolonial) linguistic conundrum: the problem of representing on the page the music and clarity of creolised English, which is, of course, the language his characters think, argue, make love and dream in – except when they happen to be speaking to their colonial masters or to the inheritors of the masters' linguistic standards of excellence and correct articulation. The problem is that if one is a writer from the Caribbean, one has to write both. It's a challenge that few of Channer's literary forebears, even great writers like V.S. Naipaul and Derek Walcott, have been able to meet, and few if any of his contemporaries. Perhaps only the polyphonic Caryl Phillips has solved this problem as effectively as Colin Channer.

The perennial question for Caribbean writers is how to represent creolised English (or French or Spanish) without making of it a mere dialect, a diminished version of the mother country's mother tongue – that's the problem, the postcolonial problem: to somehow use and abuse the language of the oppressor in order to both subvert the oppressor's mentality and tell a tale that's true to the teller's deepest, most intimate experience. Channer is the master of this bait-and-switch. Look at how skilfully he slips between the two kinds of diction and grammar; check his smooth moves as he slides his narrative in and out, ringing the changes from subjective to objective point of view, following the float from first person to third, simply by switching language tracks from creolised English (a Caribbean patois) to so-called standard English and back again:

But is jealous they jealous like Joseph brothers. And one day, one day – it might take awhile, but is sure to come – a blight going take this island, and they going have to come to Seville. And they going see me and ain't even know is me until I tell them. That is how much I going change.

"Mister, don't mind," she whispered to the rifleman beside her. She tapped his shoulder through the heavy wool. "Mister, don't you mind."

Without looking, he removed her hand and gently squeezed it with condolence. For her. For him. For history. For life.

"I'm sorry, miss," he muttered.

His father and his brother laughed.

"Is okay," she said. "Is awright." (Page 93)

Nobody does it better; at least nobody I know.

A few words concerning the themes of this fable. Without being reductive, it strikes me that there are three interwoven themes or conflicts being dramatised here. Moral conflicts, if you will, since this is after all a moral fable. They are dependence, trust and betrayal. Because Estrella is a trusting soul (still a child, remember), and because she can't escape being dependent – on men, on white people, on mixed race people, on people who possess the authority and power (and arms) of wealth and the law – she is betrayed over and over again. We see early on that she's got to lose that trust; she's got to become disillusioned. It's the only way she can protect herself against being exploited by others. And so the narrative is at bottom an account of the long and arduous process of becoming disillusioned. It starts at home in an impoverished fishing village, where Estrella is betrayed by her own grandparents, on whom she depended and whom she trusted to keep and protect her, and ends in the capital city of Seville, where she finally is somebody, regardless of her station in life, because she can no longer be fooled. She says to the white man who has just offered her a job and a home:

> "*I ain't want to wear you wife old shoes, Mr. Rawle.*
> *I walk too far from country for that. I need a ride to Salan's.*
> *I need to buy my own."*
>
>   "*I thought you didn't have any money."*
>
>   "*I lost it. But is your fault, so you going have to give me*
> *back fourteen pounds and fifty pence." Then she remembered*
> *the money from Wilfredo, whom she thought of as Simón.*
> *"Plus twenty pounds on that."*
>
>   "*That's a lot."*
>
>   "*That's my point."*
>
>   "*I don't know if I have that."*
>
>   "*If you ain't have it, put me out." (Page 122)*

Now that is no easily duped girl talking; not anymore. That is a woman to contend with.

Finally, it might be asked if we should add *The Girl with the Golden Shoes* to that short list of American classics I mentioned earlier, *The Old Man and the Sea*, *The Bear*, and so on. It's unfair to compare it to those great and finally incomparable works, as this is the work of a relatively young writer still mapping the shape of his imagination, and consequently there is here and there the occasional stylistic tentativeness one associates with such a writer. Nonetheless, his standards for his book are set as high as those set by the American masters of an earlier generation, and that is how great literature gets made. Give thanks and praise, then. This man, Colin Channer, is clearly in the business of helping make great literature.

Praise For Colin Channer

"Channer has become one of the most significant literary figures in the Caribbean, influencing writers in the islands and those living and working abroad."

—*Globe and Mail* (Canada)

For *WAITING IN VAIN*

"The love story is interesting, but not the most compelling element of the novel: What is most intriguing is the assurance of the voice, the strength of characterization, and the clear redefinition of the Caribbean novel – in which the discourses of post-colonialism have been usurped by the creative assurance of reggae's aesthetic – a quintessentially modern aesthetic that has finally found the kind of dialogue between popular music and art that we have not seen in a long time."

—*Washington Post Book World*

"Colin Channer believes fiction should 'provide a cinematic experience for the mind.' *Waiting in Vain* is a vividly sophisticated story of love and deep desire set in lush Jamaica, London's gritty Brixton, and frenetic New York."

—*Philadelphia Inquirer*

"The hope and pain of loves lost and loves found are just some of the novel's triumphs. This one just might become a best-seller."

—*Booklist*

"Channer's prose is infused with serious Caribbean lilt – the patois is perfectly rendered – and heavy, heavy love vibes. *Waiting in Vain* is what happens when a gifted writer decides to get romantic."

—*Time Out New York*

"First novelist Channer reveals his characters' idiosyncrasies in poetic description ... The culture and backdrop are so finely scripted that readers will feel they are in Jamaica."

—*Library Journal*

"Fire and Sylvia pursue and retreat from each other in convincingly soul-searching scenarios while Channer vividly describes urban New York, industrial Brixton, and rural Jamaica."

—*Publishers Weekly*

"Channer is a writer endowed with a special gift of language; he possesses a painter's eye ... Like Jean Toomer, Channer knows how to tap the rhythm of the pastoral without becoming too somnolent; and unlike the traditional novels of the past, *Waiting in Vain* is a witty, contemporary book full of well-developed, believable characters."

—*Amsterdam News*

"Caribbean in origin but global in vision, Colin Channer is Bob Marley with a pen instead of a Gibson guitar. In *Waiting in Vain*, we see an enviable and unusual achievement in the best writers – that delicate balance between poetic elegance, narrative momentum, and intellectual grace."

—Kwame Dawes, award-winning author of *Bob Marley: Lyrical Genius*

"... charged with lyrical sensuality, emotional intensity, and fearless honesty."

—*Philadelphia Tribune*

For *PASSING THROUGH*

"Channer is a gifted storyteller. He marshals the weighty themes of love, sex, race, class, and progress into an epic and vibrant narrative."

—*Washington Post*

"A splendid collection by one of the Caribbean Diaspora's finest writers. These tales are masterful distillations that teem with humor, with passion, with hope. Channer's compassion never fails to amaze."

—Junot Díaz, author of *Drown*

"Colin Channer is a wonderfully funny, piercing, crafty, and compassionate writer, and *Passing Through* is a remarkable literary achievement. The stories bring with them the keen thrill of having discovered a truly fresh, original voice – Channer's multiform vision of the Caribbean and the people who flow in and out of it is an exciting and even vital contribution to the world of the short story."

—Dan Chaon, National Book Award finalist

"No one describes the wonders and aches of love as sensuously as Colin Channer, and Channer has no rival when it comes to capturing the rhythmic beauty of island patois on the page. In *Passing Through*, Channer's silky prose is at its absolute finest; the stories are interwoven like a tapestry, a tapestry which scans across the panorama of Caribbean history to create an entirely new vocabulary of love, loss, and discovery."

—ZZ Packer, PEN/Faulkner Award finalist

"*Passing Through* takes you to the islands, into the nitty-gritty of being an islander, and the taste of being in the Caribbean. And Colin Channer's smooth Jamaican rhythm comes through his sentences. If you can't take a trip, take this as a little taste."

—Touré, author of *The Promised Land*

"Jumping into *Passing Through*, the third book by Jamaican-American author Colin Channer, is akin to visiting a foreign country and sampling its exotic cuisine and unique culture. It is an experience that teaches, entertains, and affirms the universality of our collective human experience. The communication of that shared experience, in all its perplexing, often disturbing beauty, is what Channer has clearly mastered here."

—*Virginian-Pilot*

"*Passing Through* is the story of the Caribbean depicted in all its fertile splendor by a writer whose ambition has been to attempt in writing what the region's musicians have accomplished with sound."

— Caribbean Review of Books

"Channer exhibits a remarkable ability to depict intimacy between black men and women. Probably no other novelist writing today produces such genuine and intoxicating portraits of black lovers. Indeed, it is difficult to find images of loving black couples anywhere in the media today."

— Globe and Mail (Canada)

For *IRON BALLOONS*

"The story comes at you with hurricane force and an irresistible title, 'How to Beat a Child the Right and Proper Way.' It is the creation of the Jamaican writer Colin Channer, who is also the editor of *Iron Balloons*, an anthology of a new kind of Jamaican writing ... 'The Right and Proper Way' is a big breath of a piece, fifty-four pages long, and something of a tour de force, spoken in various registers of Jamaican English."

— New York Times

"The pick of the collection is Channer's own contribution. 'How to Beat a Child the Right and Proper Way' is a hilariously digressive monologue delivered by a Jamaican woman to a class of mature students in the United States ... At first she seems to be an interfering tyrant; but her moving tale unravels to show a sympathetic, contradictory person."

— Times Literary Supplement (UK)

"The ability to eloquently delineate a particular experience – Caribbean life – accounts in large part for the significance and success of *Iron Balloons* ... The anthology offers some of today's most prominent Caribbean writers, including Kwame Dawes, Elizabeth Nunez, and Channer himself, as well as such newcomers as Marlon James and Sharon Leach."

— Toronto Star (Canada)

"The stories share a focus on lushly drawn, believably human characters, while their settings and moods are pleasingly diverse."

—Boston Herald

"Channer's 'How to Beat a Child the Right and Proper Way' is a mesmerizing tale told in a sparkling vernacular."

—Time Out Chicago

"Channer's imagery is so vivid that the brutal whipping depicted in his story can almost be heard. But Channer allows the beater – a mother straddling the working- and middle-class worlds who is disciplining her rebellious teen daughter to save her from certain destruction – to gain sympathy as she considers class, skin color, and social standing in postcolonial Jamaica."

—Philadelphia Inquirer

The Macmillan Caribbean Writers Series

Series Editor: Jonathan Morley

Look out for other exciting titles from the region:

Crime thrillers:

Rum Justice   *Jolien Harmsen*

Fiction:

The Festival of San Joaquin: *Zee Edgell*

The Voices of Time: *Kenrick Mose*

She's Gone: *Kwame Dawes*

John Crow's Devil: *Marlon James*

This Body: *Tessa Mcwatt*

Walking: *Joanne Allong Haynes*

Trouble Tree: *John Hill Porter*

Power Game: *Perry Henzell*

Short Stories:

The Fear of Stones: *Kei Miller* (shortlisted for the 2007 Commonwealth Writers' Prize)

Poetry:

Poems of Martin Carter: *Stewart Brown And Ian Mcdonald (eds.)*

Selected Poems of Ian Mcdonald: *Edited By Edward Baugh*

Plays:

Bellas Gate Boy (includes Audio CD) :   *Trevor Rhone*

Two Can Play: *Trevor Rhone*